To Becca!
A Real TRUE
Princess!

A Totally True PRINCESS STORY

Story
Chris Patton

Illustrations
Claude St. Aubin

Colors
Jamilyn!

Edited by
Mike Wellman

Layouts by
Chris Brandt

Logo Design by
Richard Starkings of Comicraft

A long time ago, even before your grandparents were born, and far away, so far away that you couldn't see it if you stood on a rainbow, there was a place…

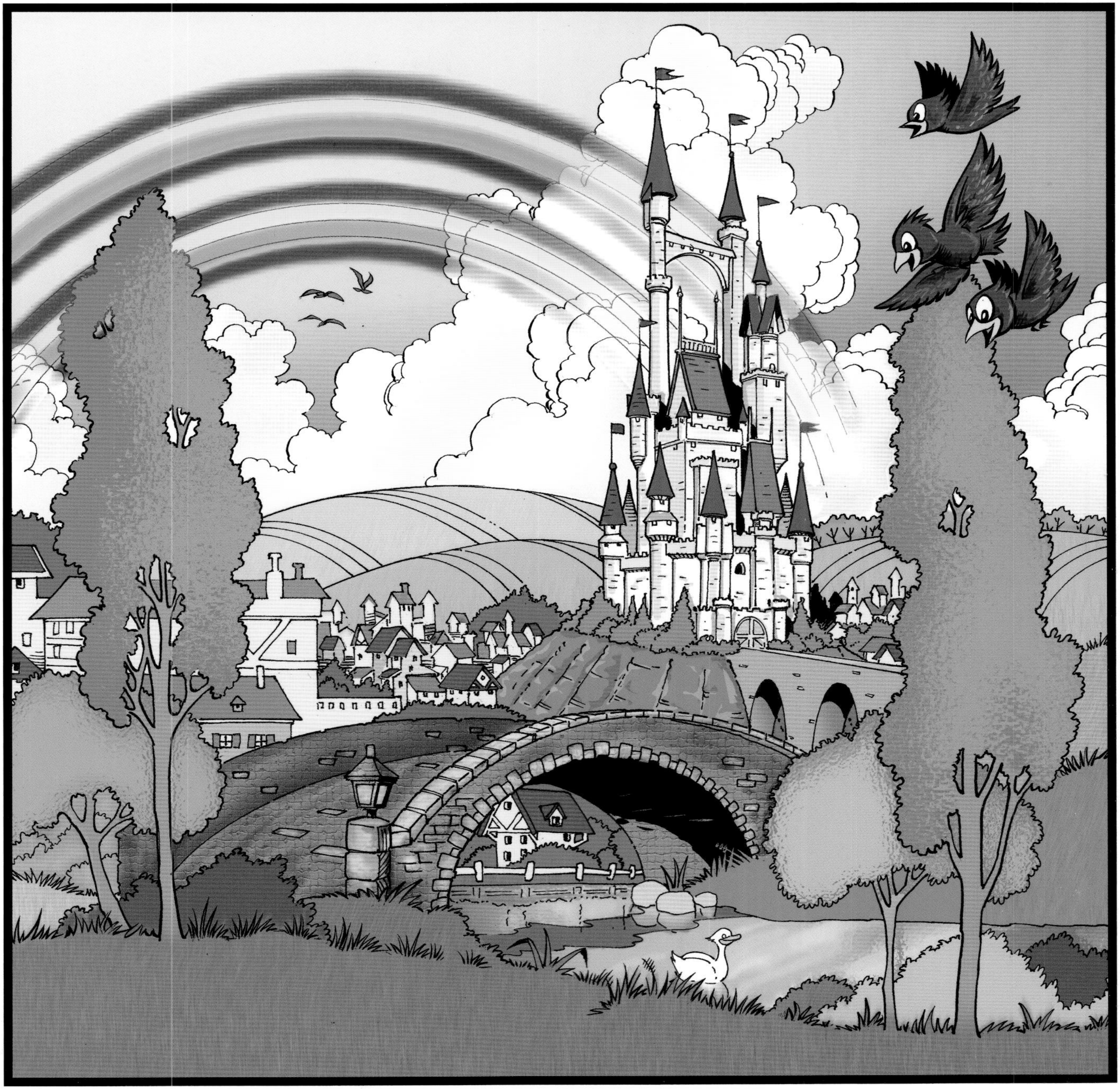

This place was known as the Kingdom of HooHooHaHa. It was truly wonderful. In this land, nobody was ever mean or sick. Maybe that's because it was always summertime and nobody ever went to school. All anybody ever ate was hot dogs, which grew on trees. All they drank was strawberry milk, which came from pink cows.

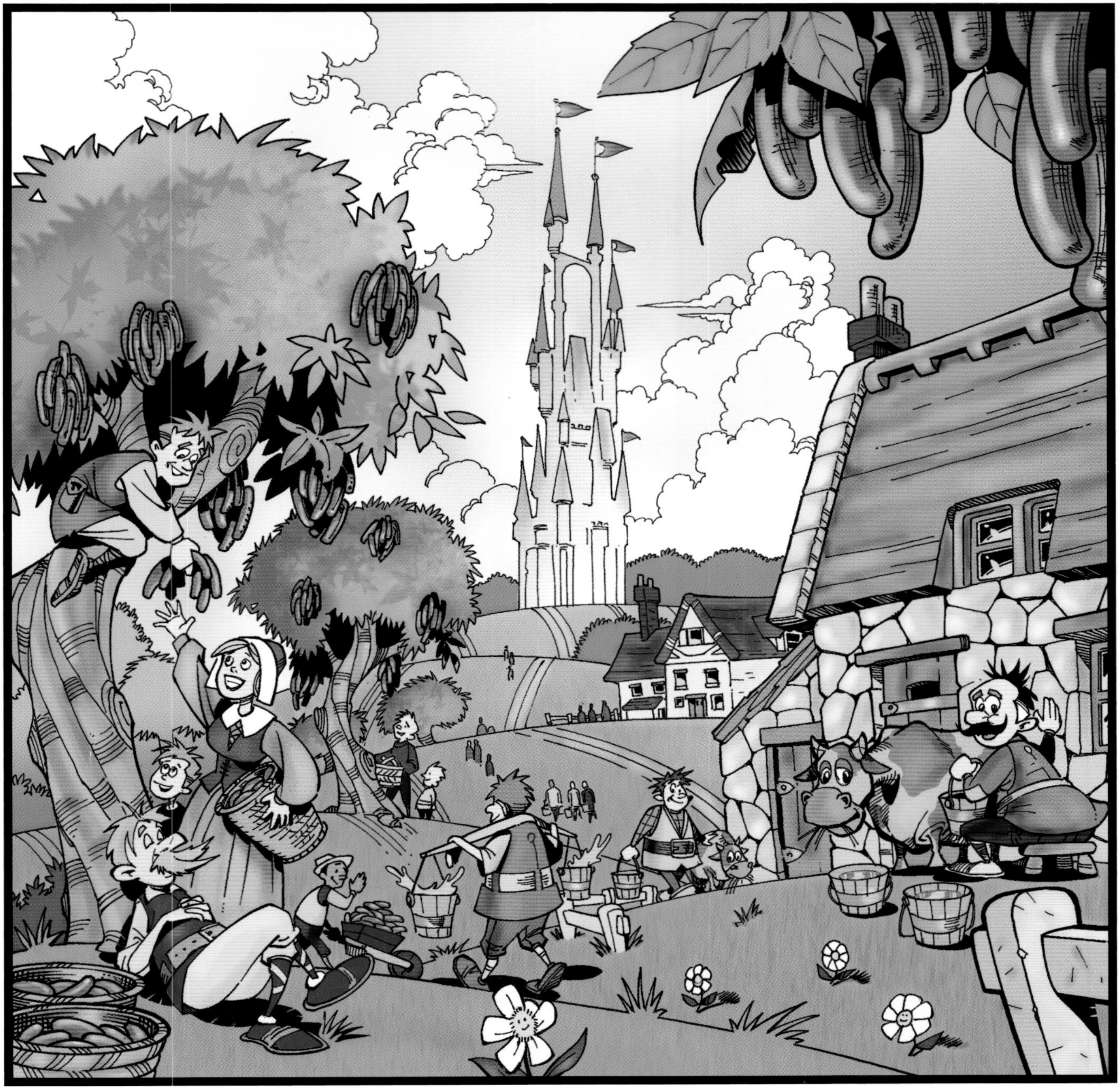

Frankie and Sasha, two of the fairest Princesses that ever were, ruled over HooHooHaHa. Frankie was a little older, and Sasha a little younger, but they were best of friends. They were beautiful and kind and smart and tough (but only when they had to be). No wonder the people of HooHooHaHa loved them!

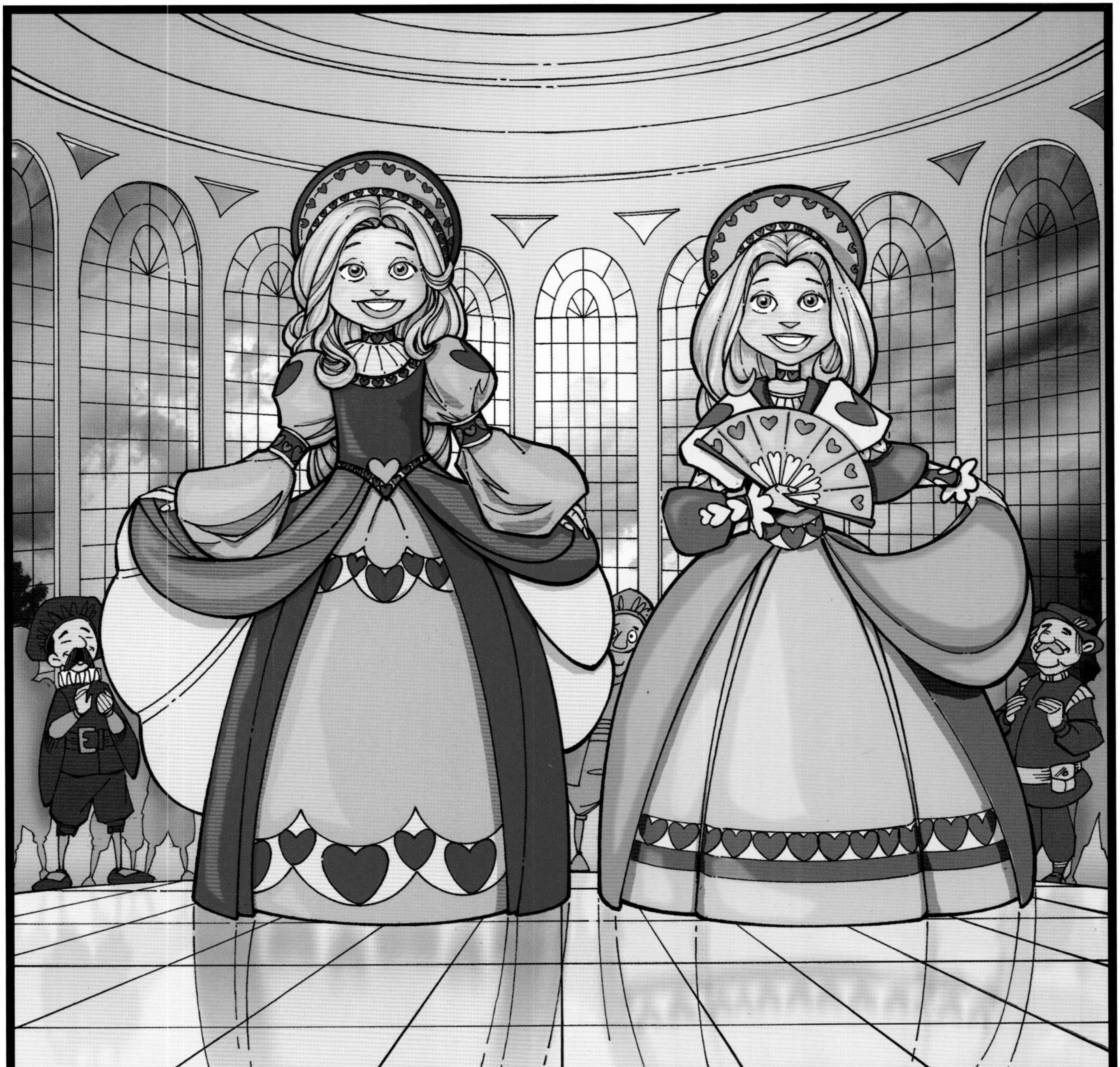

Did I mention that HooHooHaHa was a magical place? I didn't? Well, there was magic everywhere! Mostly, it was the good kind of magic, like when a baby smiles or a flower blooms, but there was just enough of the bad kind of magic to cause trouble.

Almost all of this bad magic was in the hands of a woman so awful and nasty that she was known only as the Mean Queen. She ruled the neighboring Kingdom of Vile.

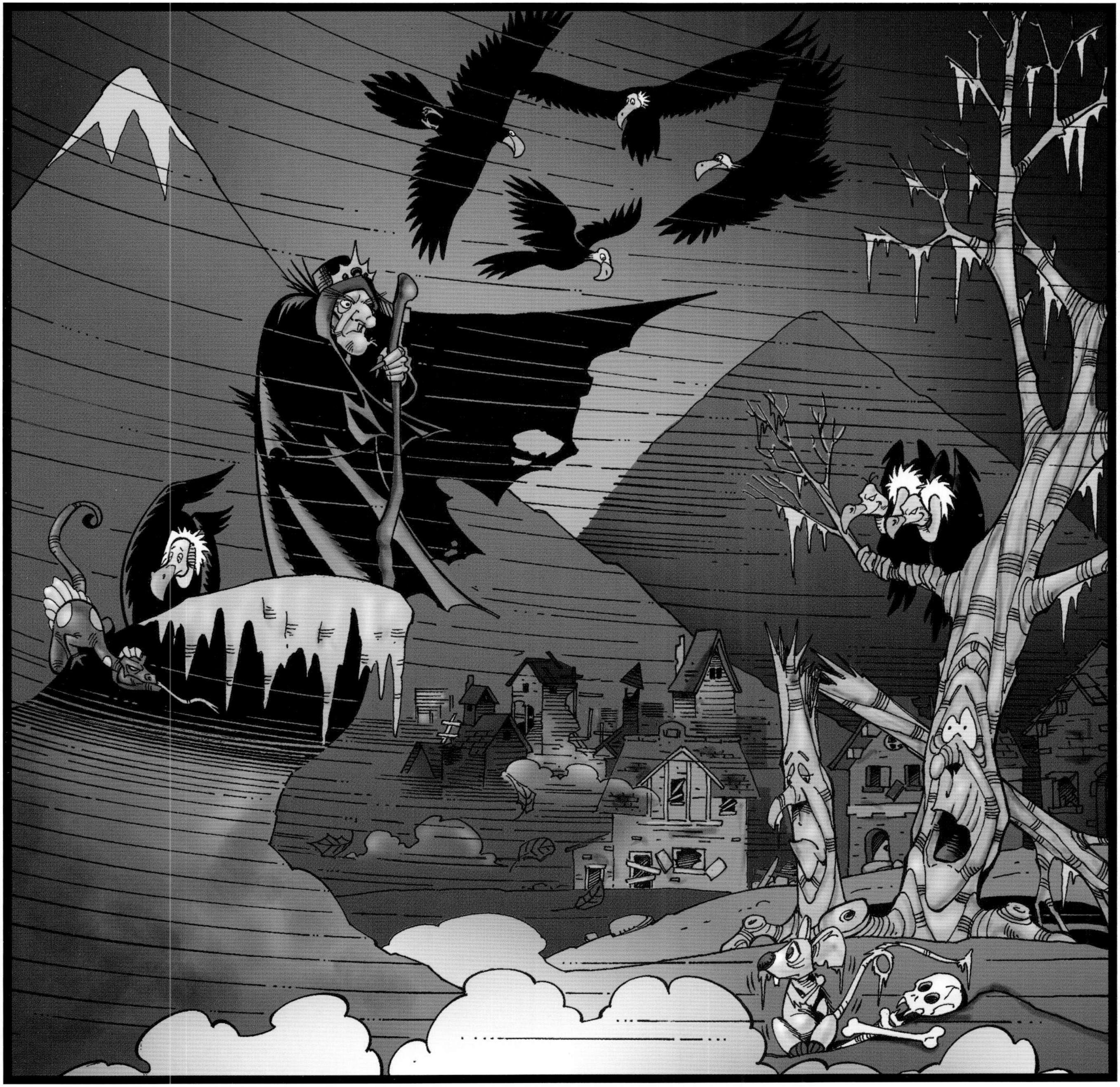

Things there were so bad that all of the people had moved to HooHooHaHa, leaving the Mean Queen all alone. The Mean Queen hated everything and everyone and was always angry about something. Whenever she got extra angry or bored, which was pretty often, she would cast a spell and conjure an army of monsters or some other bad thing to bring trouble to the good people of HooHooHaHa.

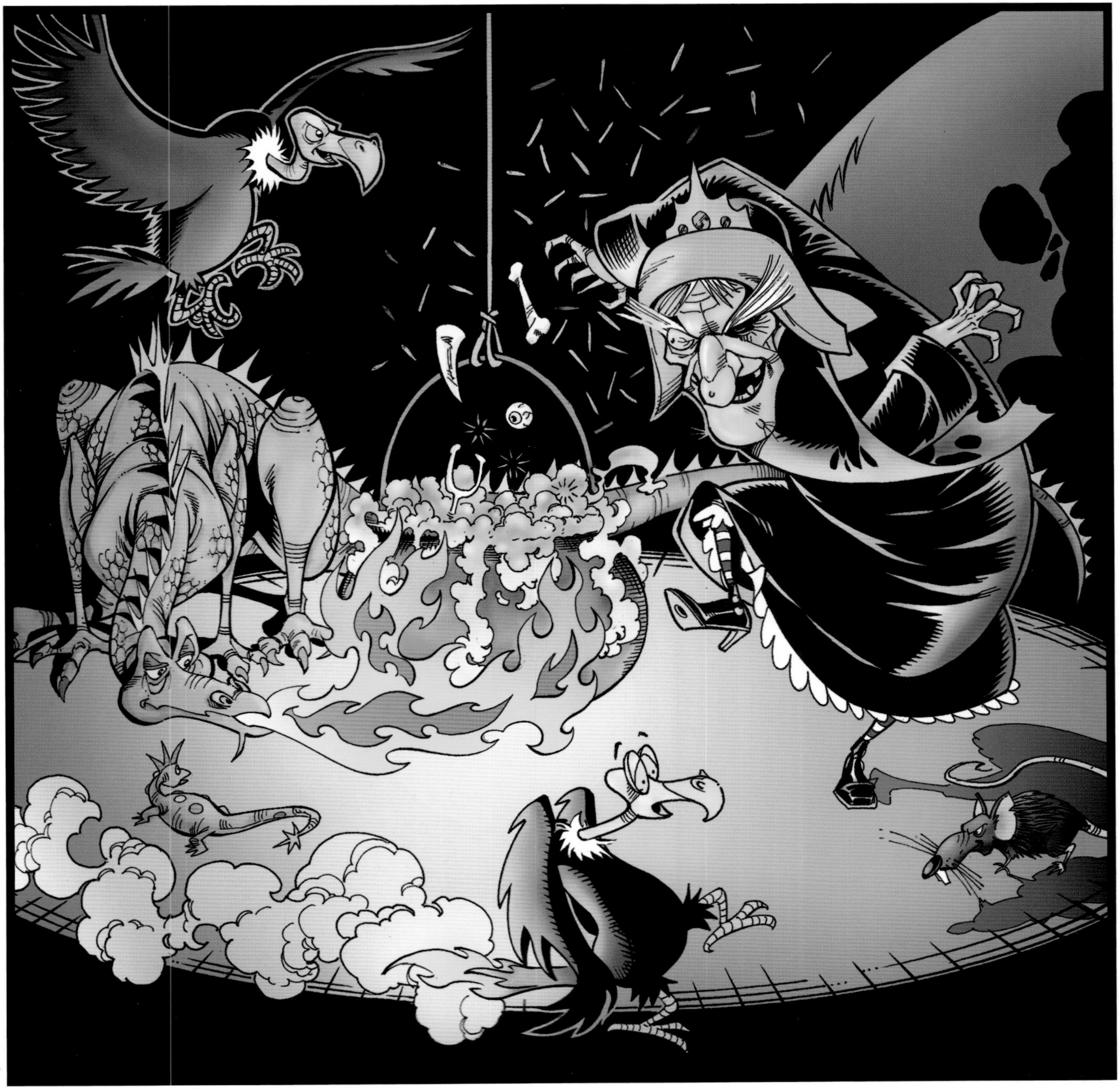

This is when Frankie and Sasha's smartness and toughness would pay off, because they would lead the HooHooHaHa army into battle against these bad things and win, every time.

Once, the Mean Queen attacked with an army of Yeti Crabs!

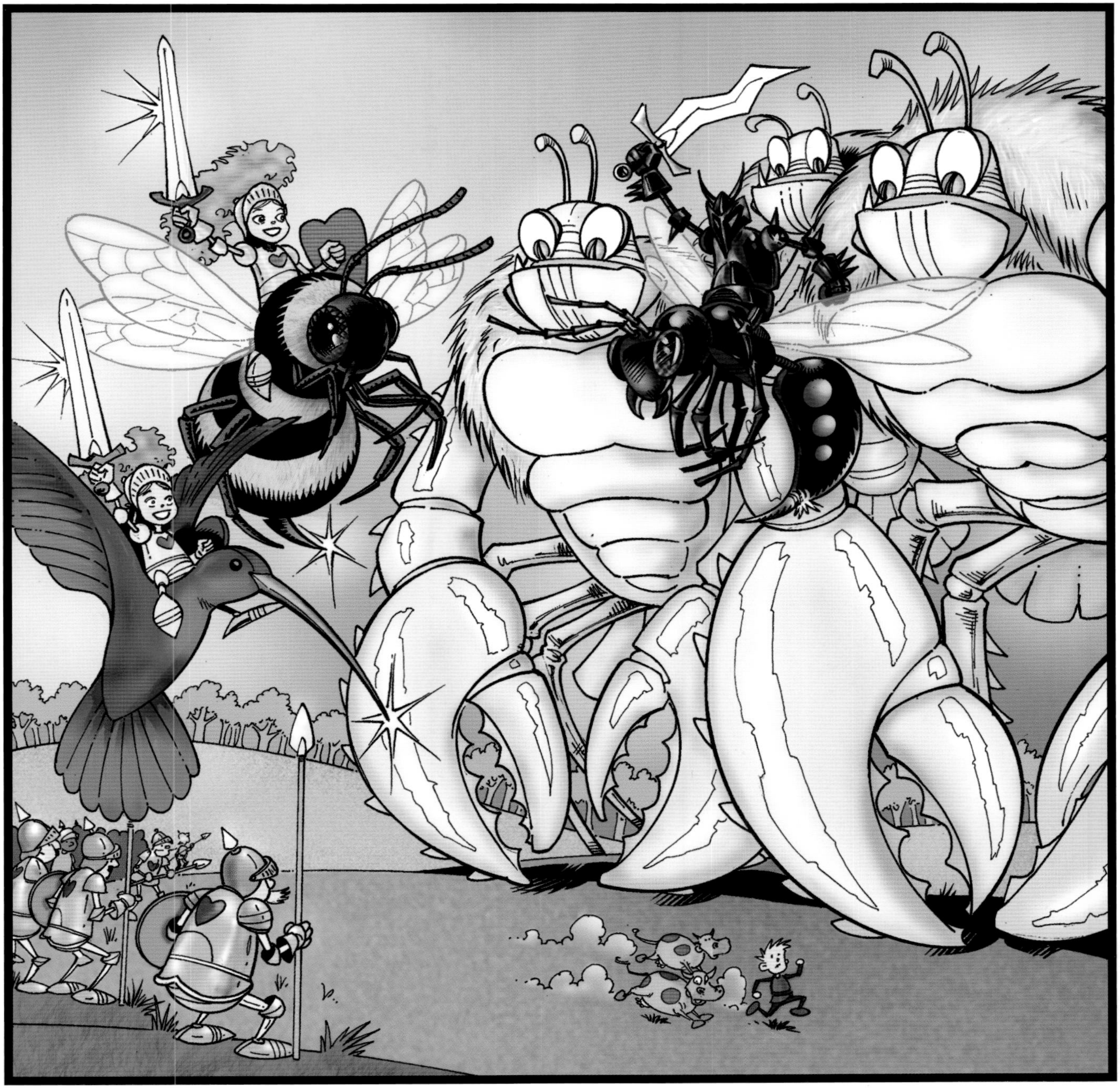

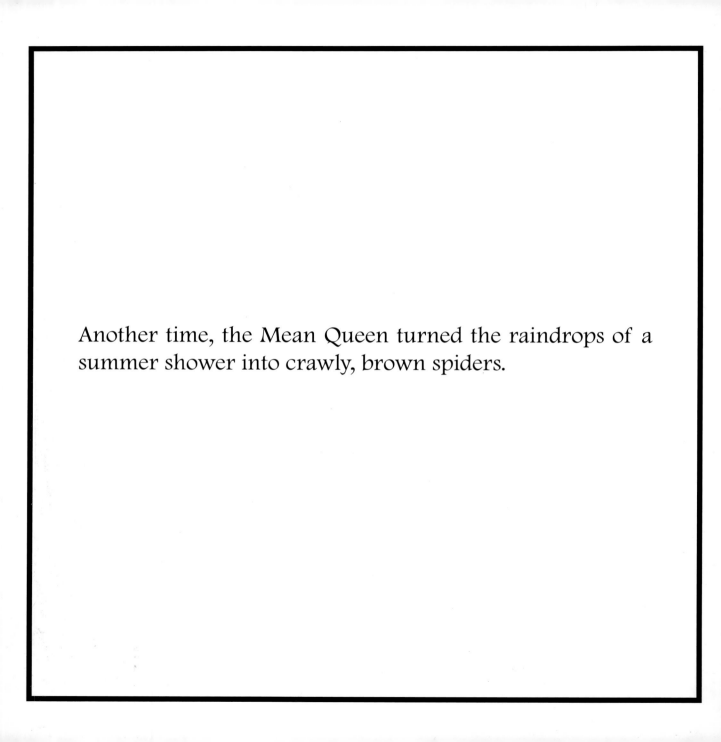

Another time, the Mean Queen turned the raindrops of a summer shower into crawly, brown spiders.

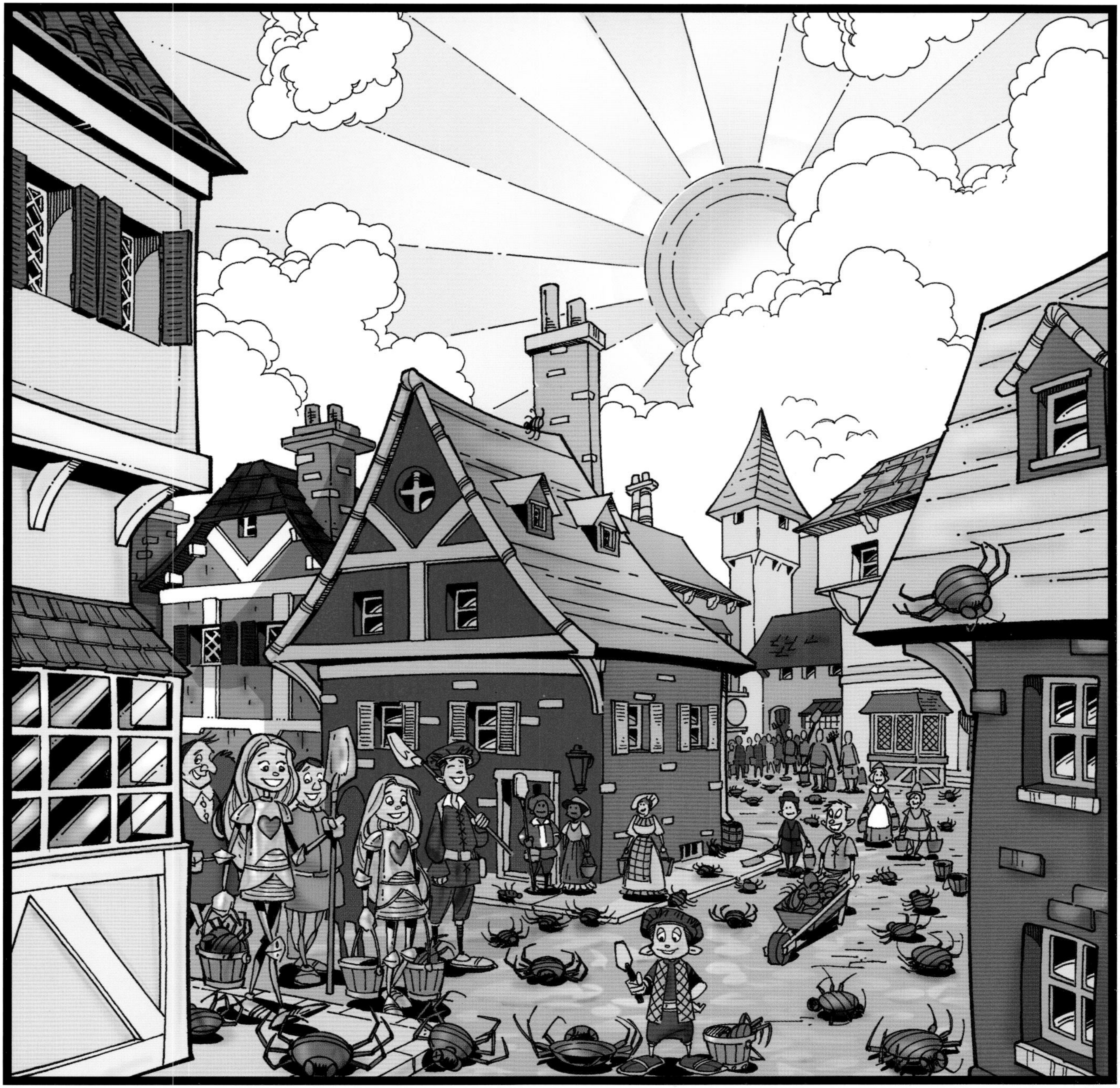

Then there was the time she sent giant flying slugs to drip slime on everyone and everything.

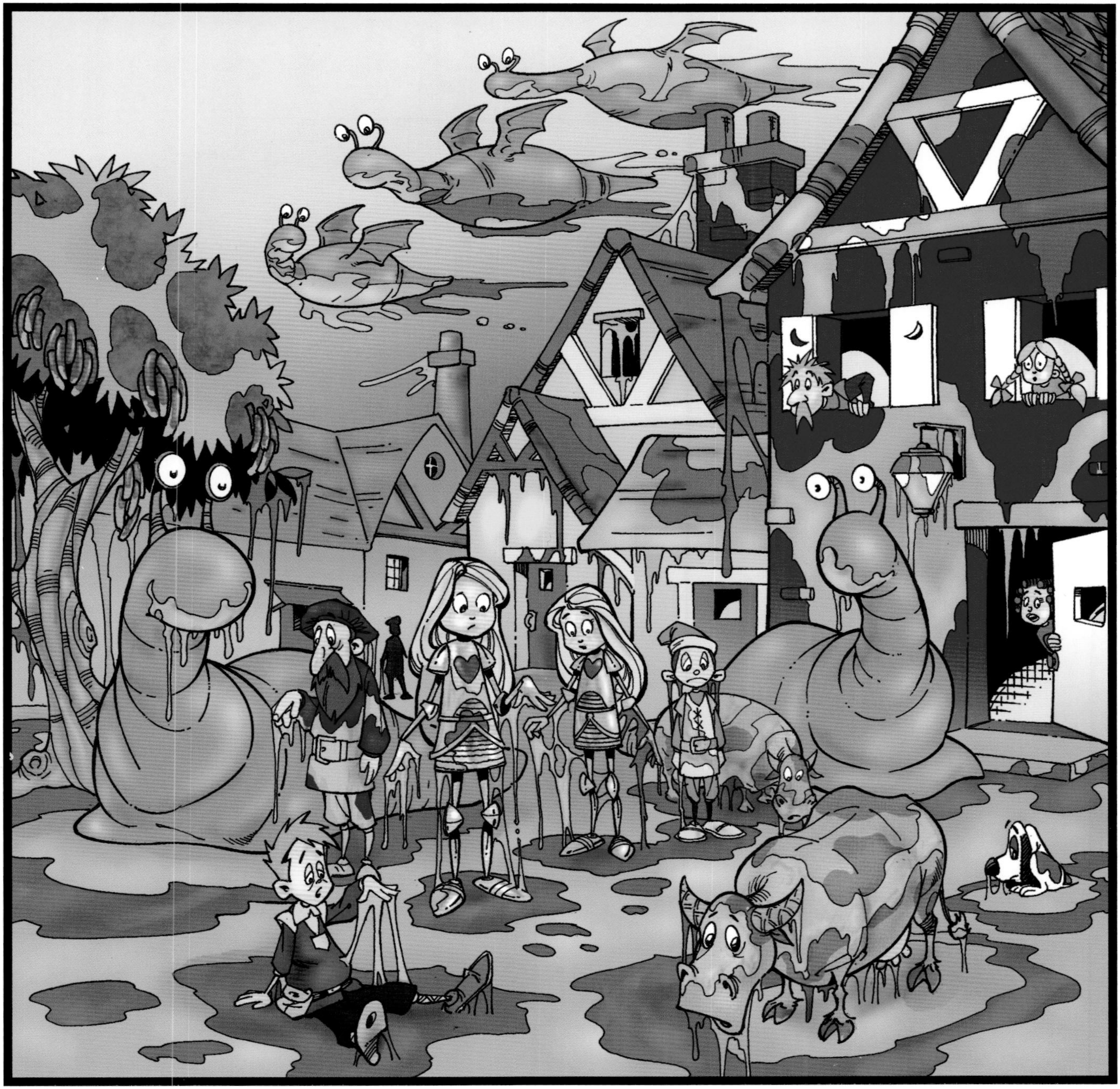

Then the Mean Queen turned all of the ice cream into lima beans.

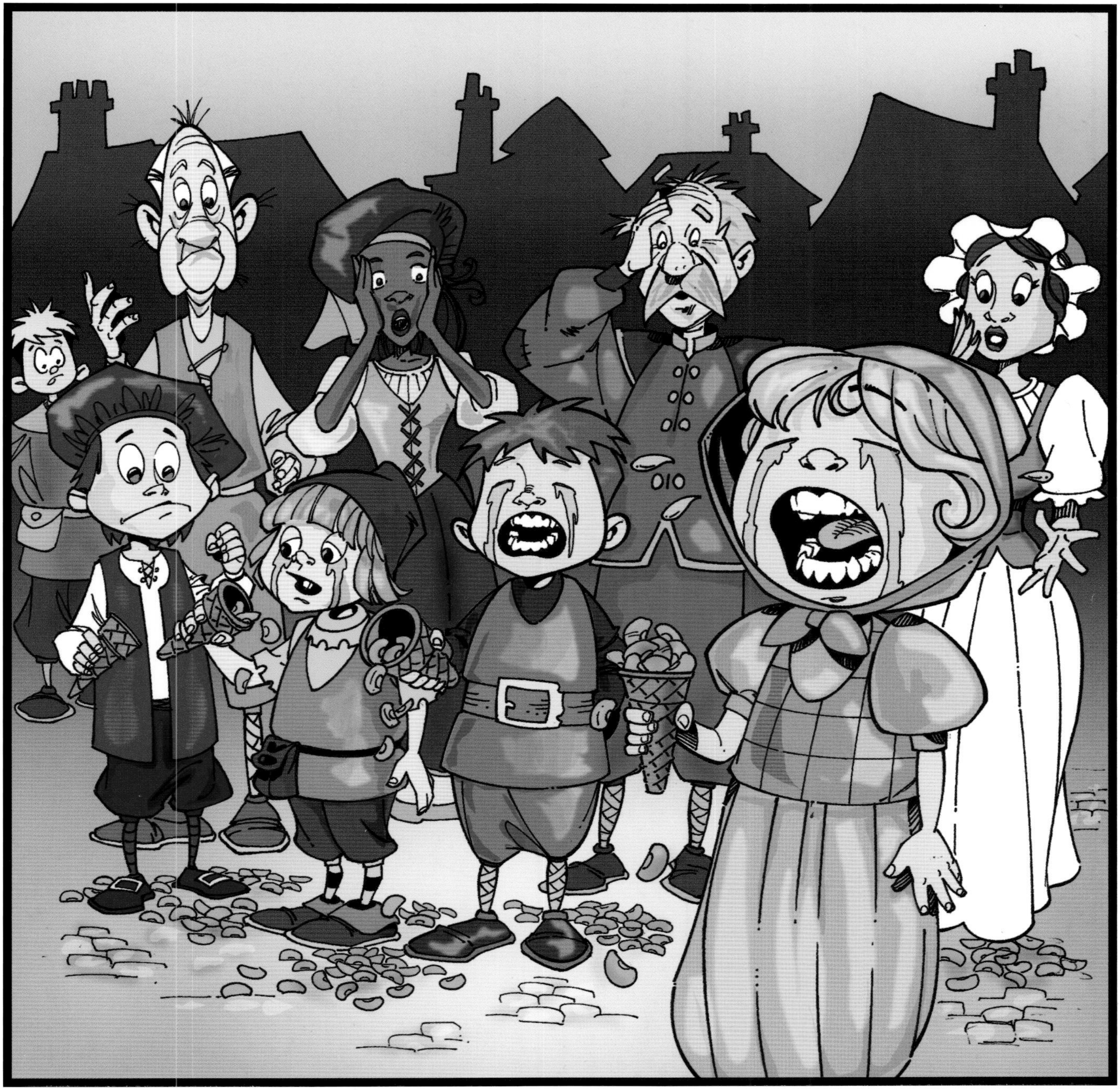

Ruining the ice cream of HooHooHaHa was the final straw for the Princesses. Fed up, they traveled to the Kingdom of Vile and captured the Mean Queen, putting an end to her reign of terror once and, hopefully, for all.

They threw the Mean Queen in a dungeon to ponder her evil ways. Well, actually, it wasn't a dungeon. It was more like a nice hotel room, except the door was locked and there was no room service or television.

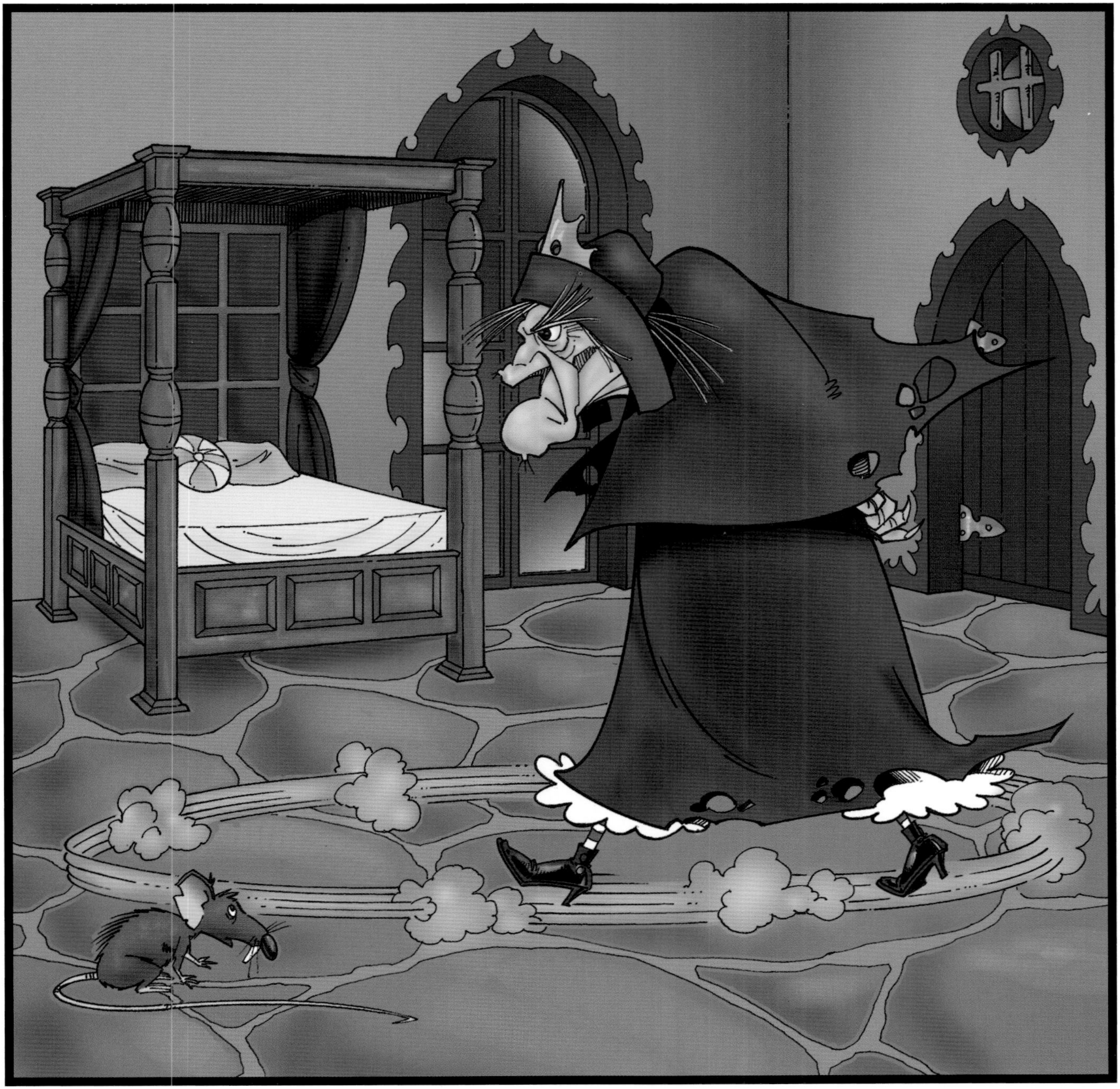

That night, the whole kingdom stayed up very late celebrating. By the time everyone finally went to bed, it was past ten o'clock!

As late as it was, Frankie still couldn't get to sleep. She was glad the Mean Queen was finally out of their hair, but she had a strange, nagging feeling that this had all happened before and would probably happen yet again. You see, she had recently realized that parts of her life didn't quite add up. She and Sasha were big girls, but she couldn't remember having a birthday. She knew that her parents were the King and Queen, but she didn't know their names. It just seemed strange somehow. She went to Sasha's room to wake her up and tell her about these troubling thoughts. Sasha agreed with her sister that things may not be as they seemed and would keep an eye out for any funny business.

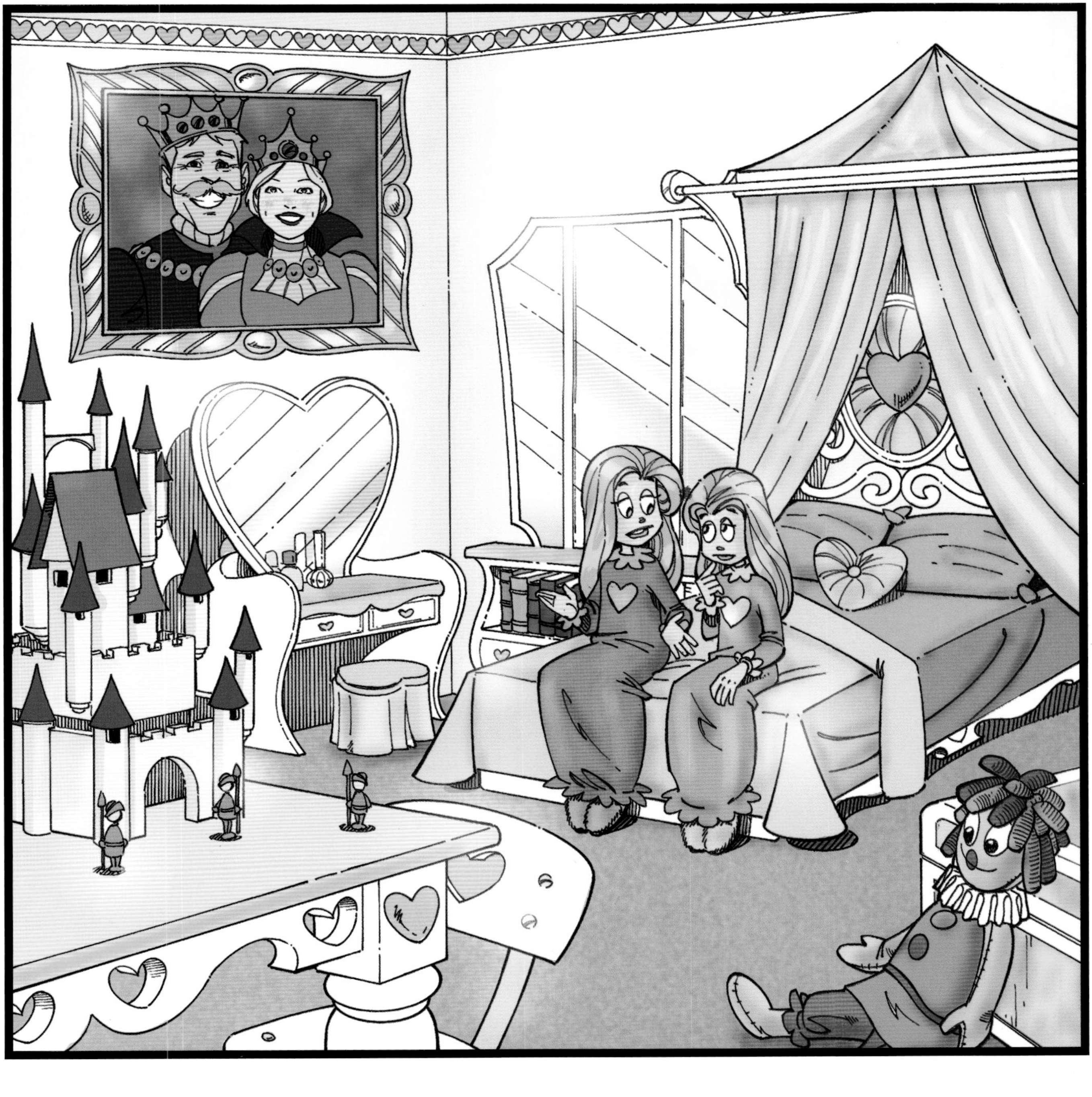

Sure enough, a few days later, the girls found themselves shoveling up spiders yet again.

"I knew it!" Frankie exclaimed.

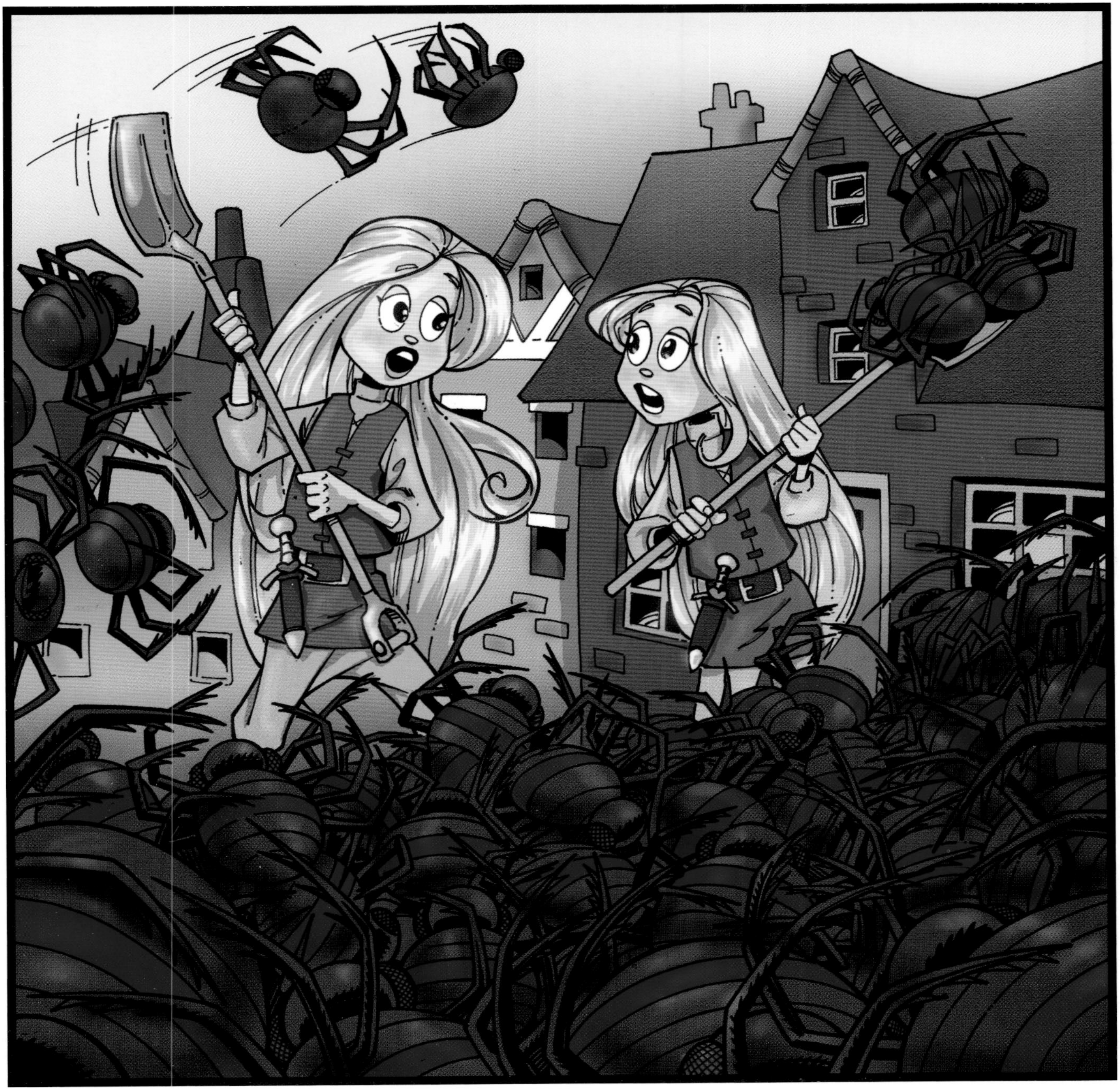

Like clockwork, the slugs and lima bean ice cream soon followed, even though the Mean Queen was still locked in the dungeon. Frankie and Sasha went to see if she had any idea why such a thing would happen.

The Mean Queen thought a bit. "Come to think of it, I don't know my real name either. And I'm not as ugly as people think." With that, she removed her mask and false nose. "In fact, I don't even like being mean! I just feel like I'm supposed to be. Something odd is definitely going on!"

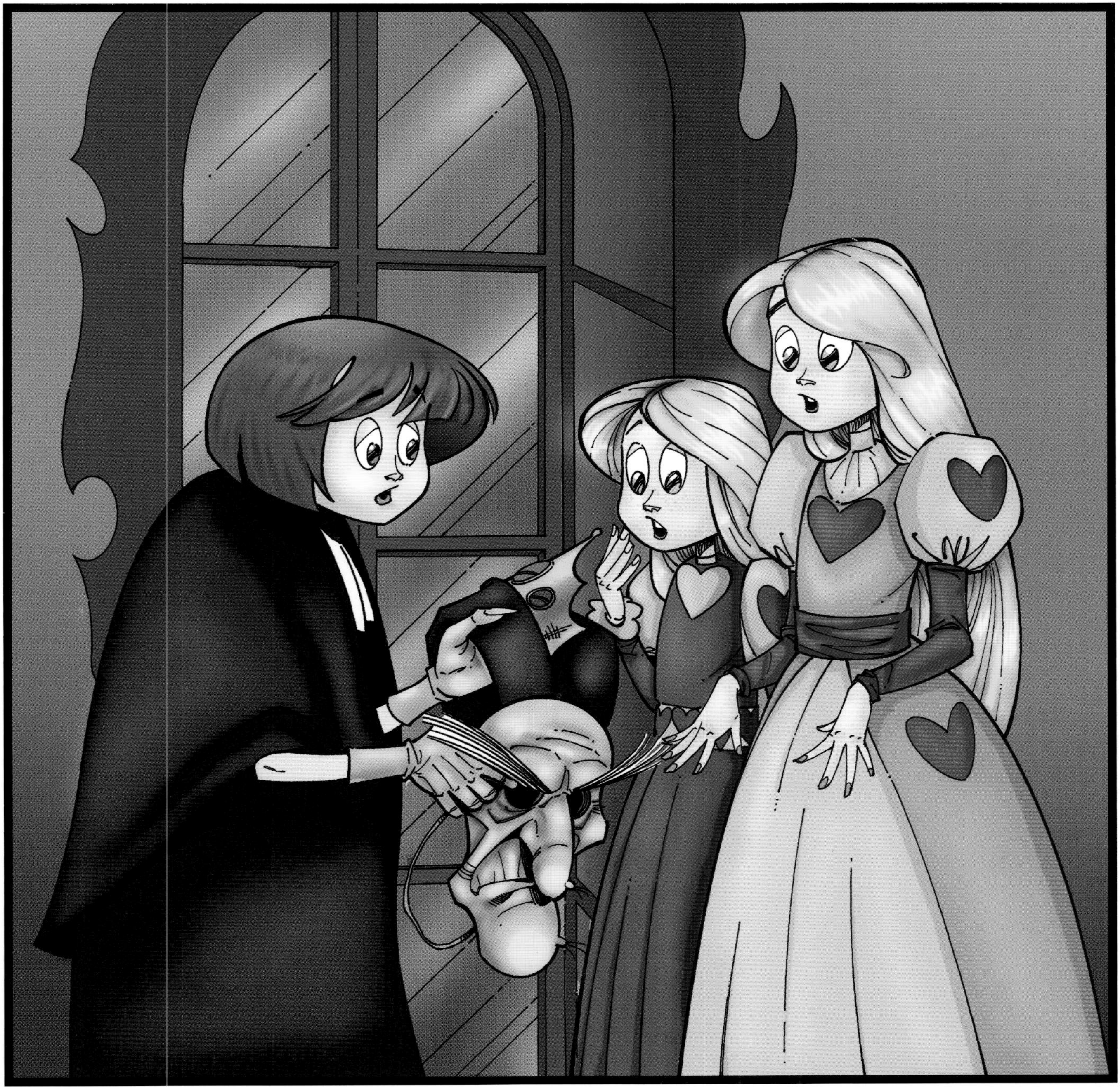

After the three girls decided to work together to solve this mystery, the Mean Queen decided she would need a new name. Her new name would be the Formerly Mean Queen until they could think of something better.

She went home to study her books of spells while Frankie and Sasha flew to the far corners of the world to gather various magical objects. They had many great adventures in their travels, but those are stories for another time.

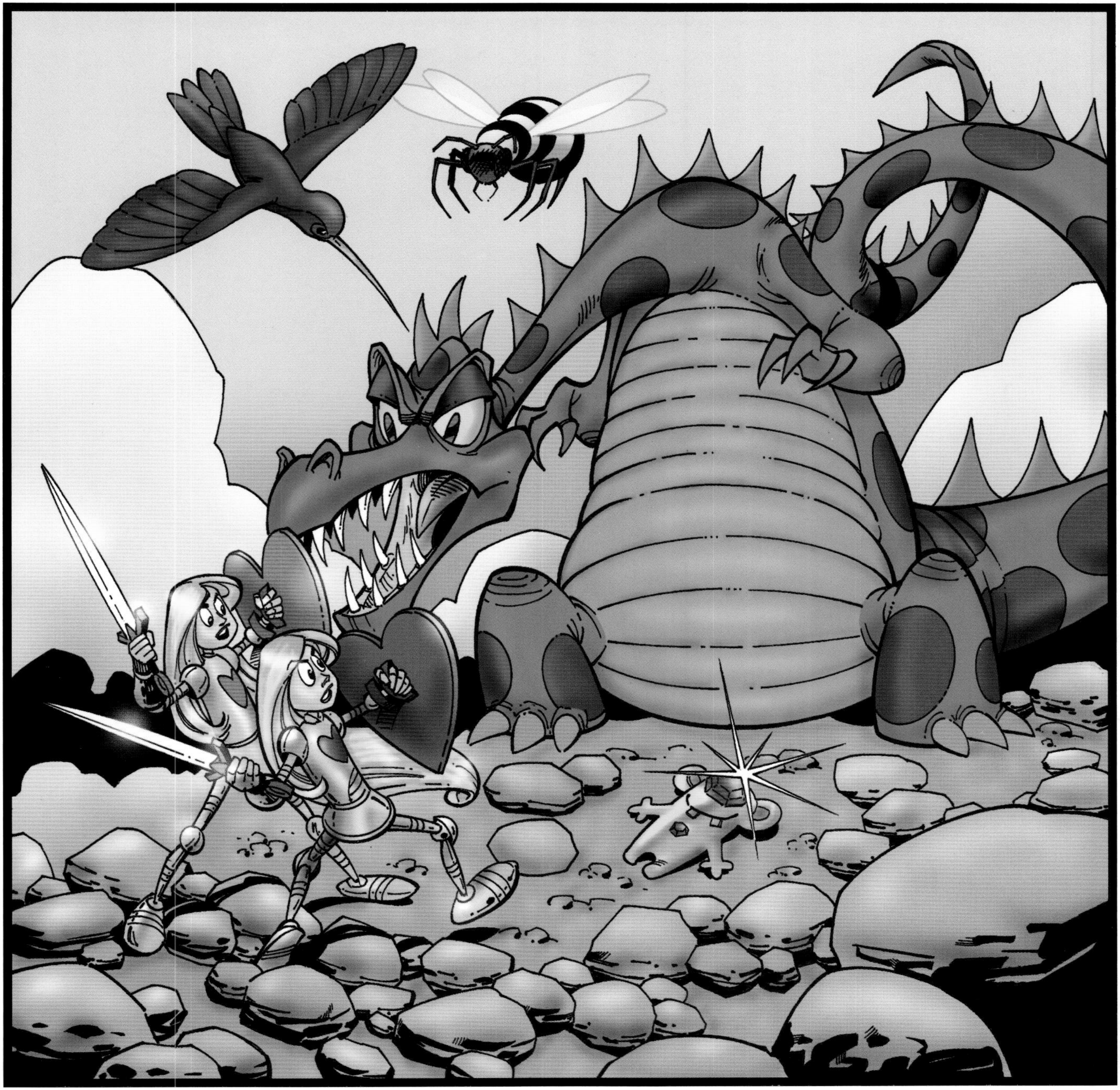

Once they had all of the items they needed, the three girls gathered in a circle while the Formerly Mean Queen cast her most powerful spell ever. The sky above them opened up with a loud zipping noise. The opening was so high in the sky that they had to fly up and squeeze through fast before it closed behind them.

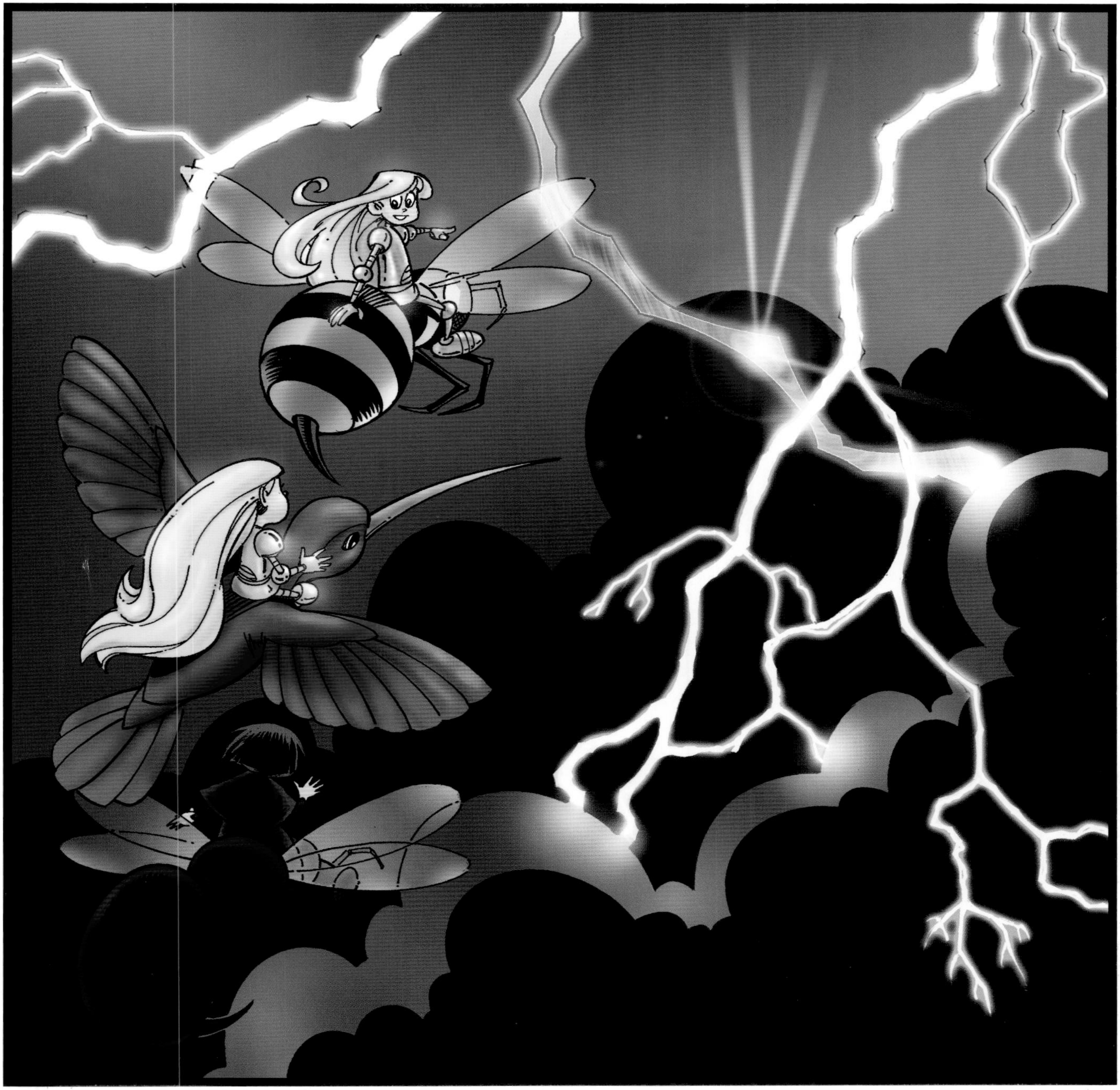

In a place very different from both HooHooHaHa and the Kingdom of Vile, there was a little girl named Tammy Turnipseed.

Little Tammy Turnipseed was sad most of the time. She had no friends and the kids at school were mean to her because she was poor and wore old clothes and brought her lunch to school in a paper sack. One boy named Max pulled her hair every day and sometimes even took her paper sack.

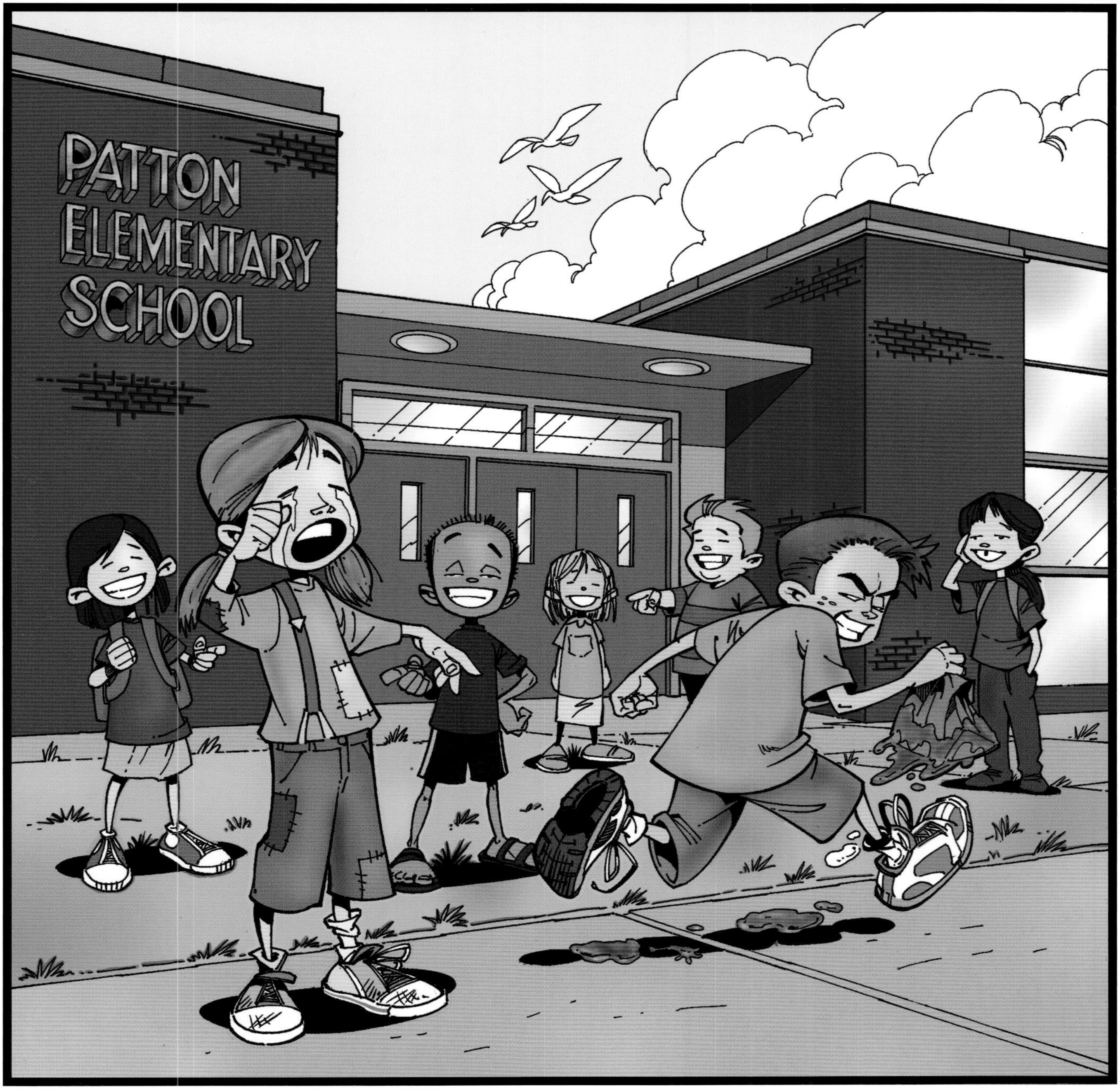
PATTON
ELEMENTARY
SCHOOL

Home wasn't much better. She didn't have any brothers or sisters. Her mom wasn't around any more. Her dad worked seven days a week at the underwear factory where he tested the elastic bands on the underwear to make sure they were stretchy enough but not too stretchy.

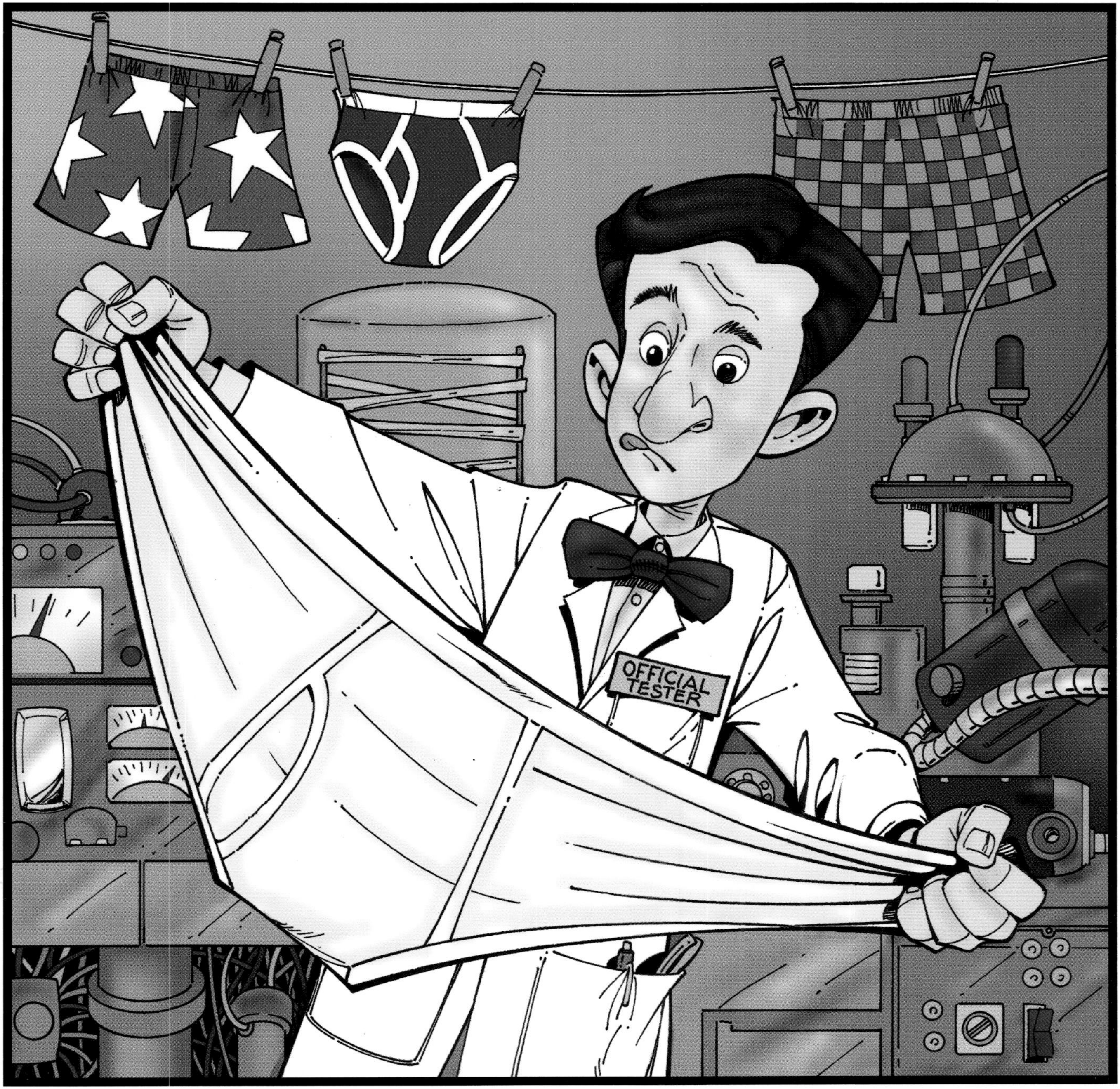
OFFICIAL TESTER

Tammy had a babysitter almost every day. Because underwear elastic testing didn't pay very much, Mr. Turnipseed could afford only the cheapest babysitter in town.

Unfortunately for Tammy, that meant she was watched by the meanest babysitter in town! This babysitter didn't even like kids! She ignored Tammy and talked on the phone all night. She wouldn't let Tammy watch the TV she wanted and ate all the treats her daddy left her. In fact, she was so mean that she would even make Tammy clean up the crumbs as she ate the cookies her daddy left her!

She only talked to Tammy to yell at her. To avoid all that meanness, Tammy spent all of her time in her room reading books and playing with the few toys she had.

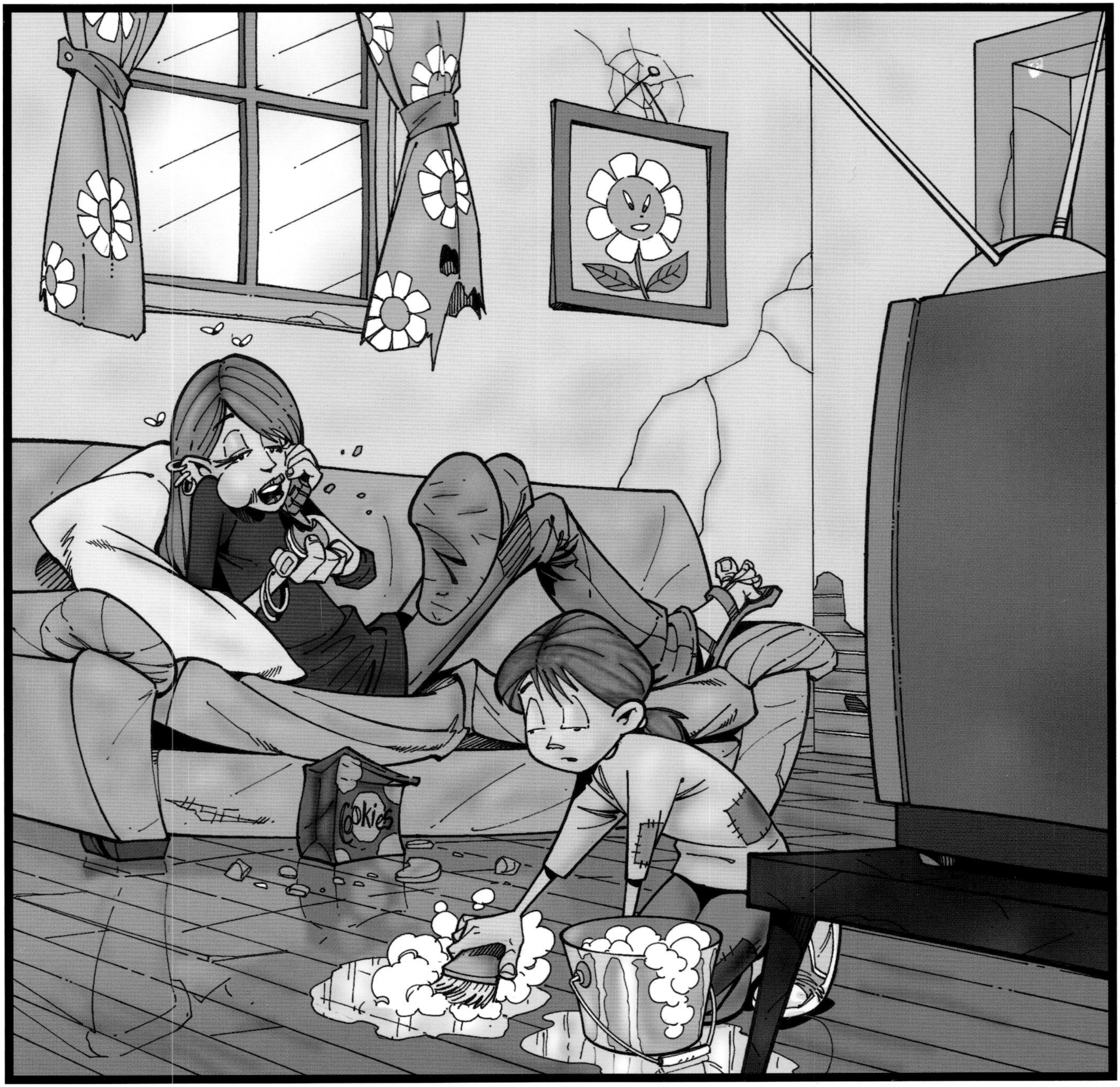
Cookies

Tammy's favorite thing in the world was to snuggle in bed with her daddy and read her favorite book. It was about two beautiful warrior princesses that flew into battle and always saved the kingdom. Sound familiar?

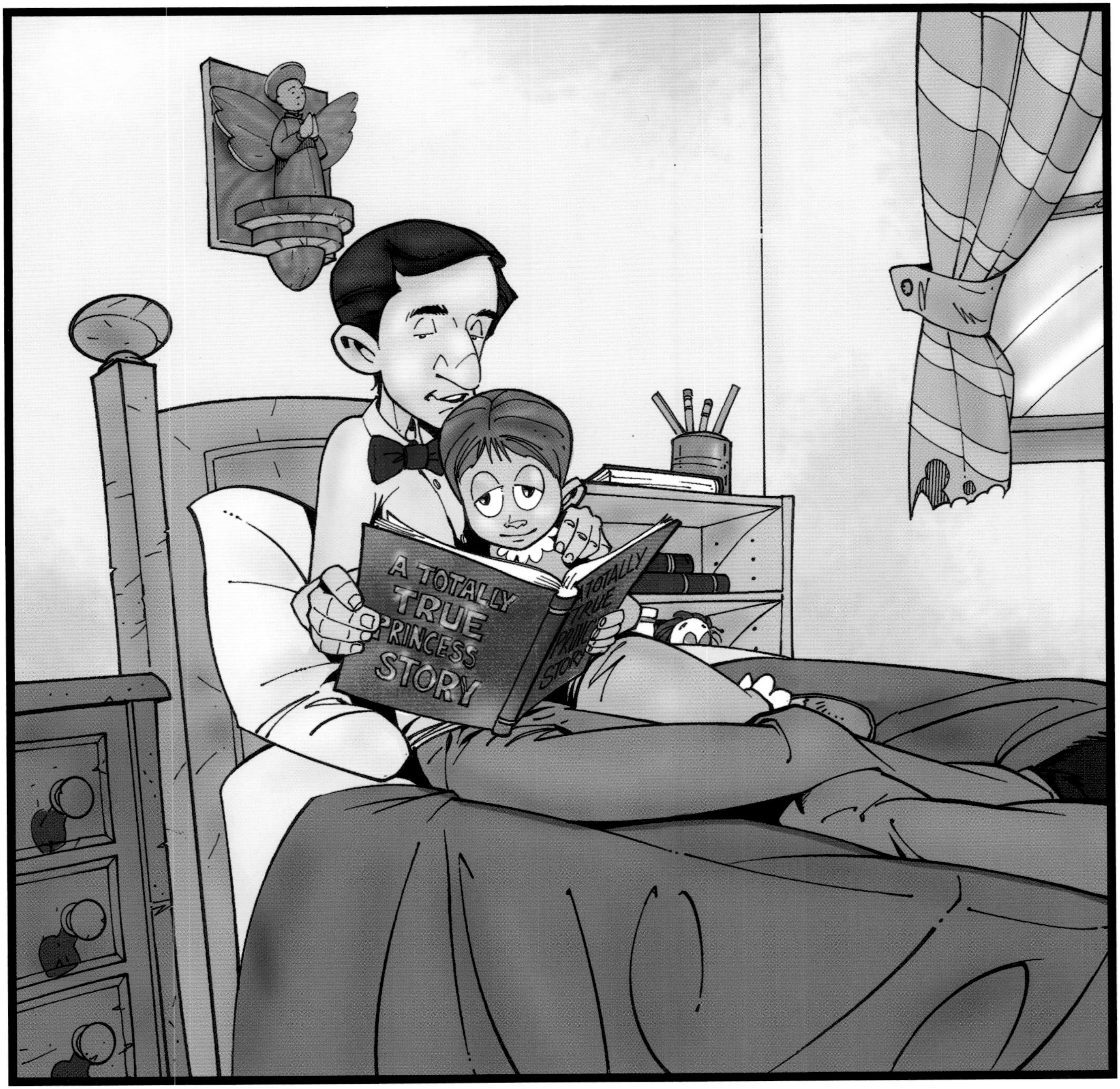
A TOTALLY TRUE PRINCESS STORY
A TOTALLY TRUE PRINCESS STORY

One afternoon, Max the bully was meaner than ever, pulling Tammy's hair and pushing her down in a mud puddle. Tammy couldn't get home fast enough. She ran past the babysitter without even saying "hi" and closed herself in her room.

Tammy noticed her favorite book had fallen off the shelf and the cover was torn. When she looked inside, she saw that the Princesses had been erased. Who would do such a cruel thing? The babysitter was mean, but she never left the couch. Had Max gotten in the house somehow? All she could do was hug the book and weep bitter tears.

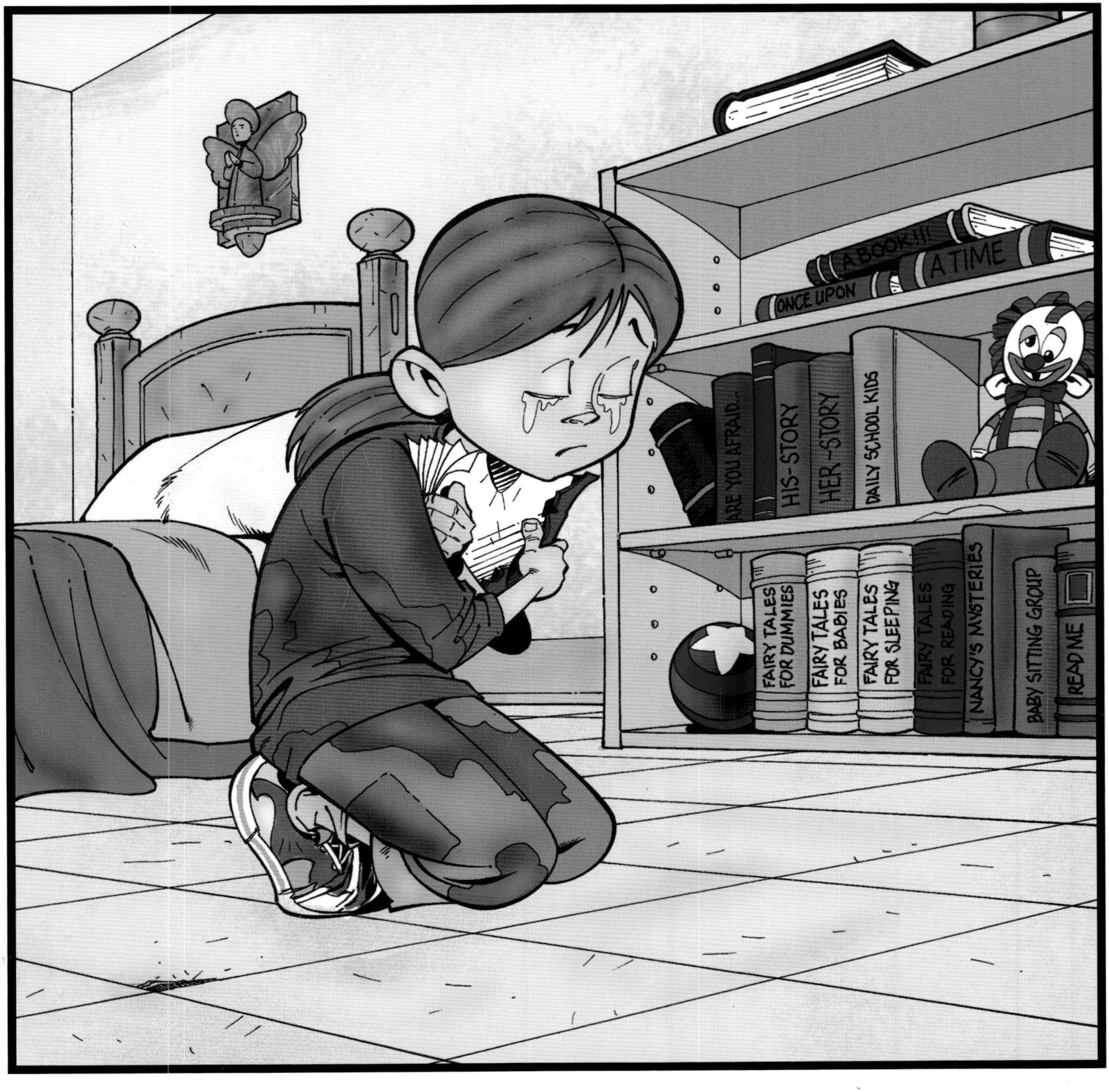
A BOOK!!!
ONCE UPON
A TIME
ARE YOU AFRAID...
HIS-STORY
HER-STORY
DAILY SCHOOL KIDS
FAIRY TALES FOR DUMMIES
FAIRY TALES FOR BABIES
FAIRY TALES FOR SLEEPING
FAIRY TALES FOR READING
NANCY'S MYSTERIES
BABY SITTING GROUP
READ ME

Frankie, Sasha and the Formerly Mean Queen were watching the little girl (who looked quite large to them) from their hiding place in the curtains. They had burst through their sky and into this realm of giants just a few minutes ago. They were confused and more than a little bit scared, to say the least. Once they heard Tammy begin to cry, they forgot all about being afraid and flew down to comfort her.

"It's all right," said Sasha.

"There, there," said Frankie.

"Don't cry little girl," said the Formerly Mean Queen, putting to rest any doubts that she was still mean. "What seems to be the matter?"

Then they tried to hug her but their arms were much too short. Instead, they held hands and half-hugged her neck.

Tammy felt something touching her and looked down. She rubbed her eyes. She had to be dreaming, but she didn't remember falling asleep. And the little people looked familiar. She rubbed her eyes some more. It couldn't be! It was Frankie, Sasha and the Mean Queen! She would have been scared of the Mean Queen if she wasn't so tiny.

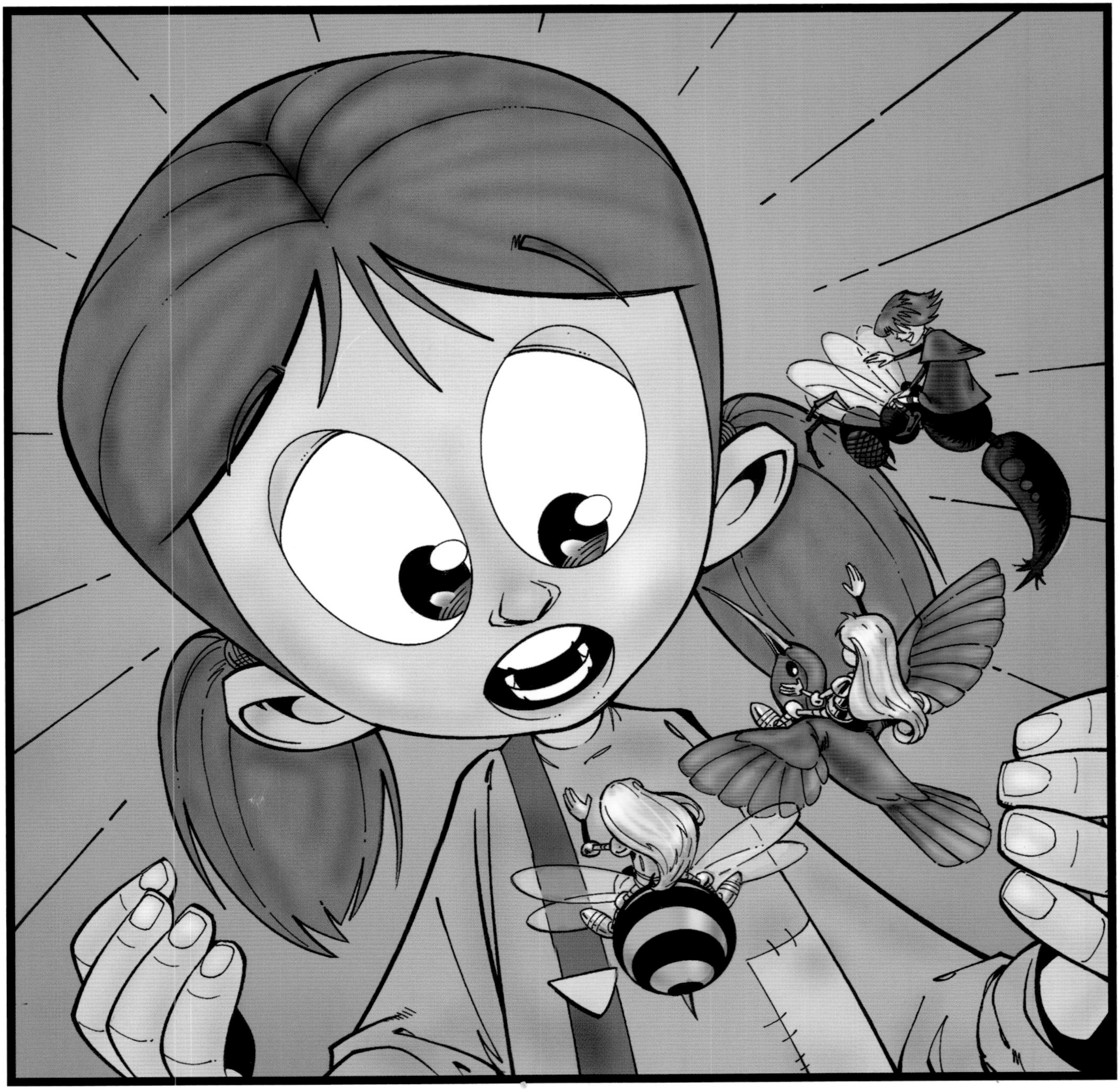

Well, if they were real, the polite thing to do was answer them.

"I was crying because you were missing from my storybook," Tammy said.

"Storybook?" Frankie replied quizzically.

Tammy told them how they were the characters right out of her favorite book. They didn't really believe her at first, but how else could she know about HooHooHaHa and all of their adventures? That would also explain how their lives kept repeating themselves.

Frankie and Sasha told Tammy how the Mean Queen was now the Formerly Mean Queen. They told her how the Formerly Mean Queen opened the hole in the sky that brought them to Tammy's world. Then, they explained to her—very nicely, so as not to hurt her feelings—that while it was nice to find out about the nature of their existence and to be out of the book, they missed their family and friends terribly and wanted to go back into the story. After all, it was their home and they were much too tiny to stay in this world!

Since these were the first friends Tammy had ever had, she told them all about herself. She told them about her Daddy, the rotten babysitter and all the mean kids at school, especially Max.

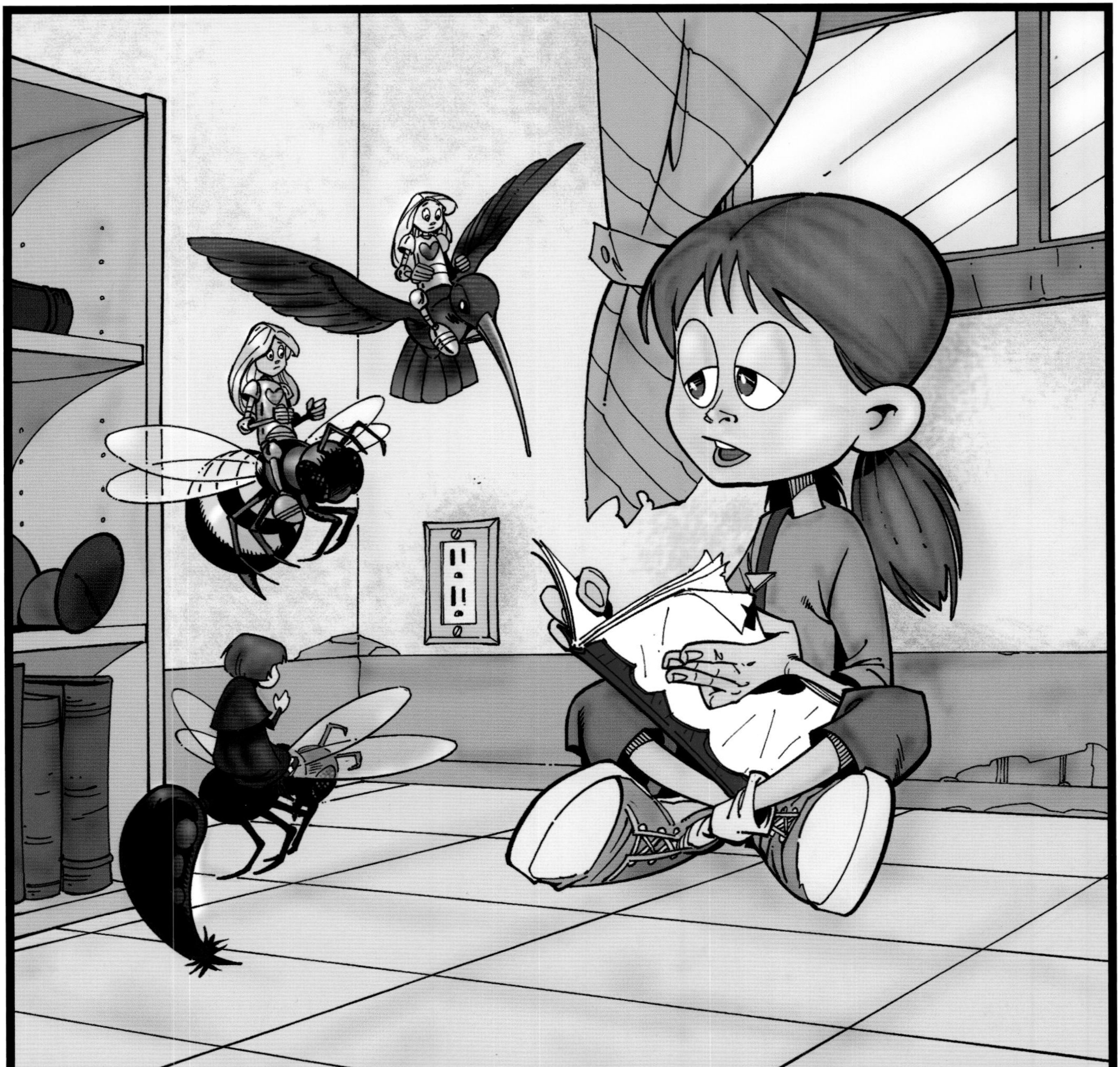

Now it was Frankie, Sasha and the Formerly Mean Queen's turn to be sad. They had thought their lives had been rough with all those evil spells and the constant fighting, but now that they knew it was all pretend, they felt lucky. Tammy's life was real, and it sounded pretty lousy.

And even though they were her best (and don't forget ONLY) friends, Tammy promised to help them get back home any way she could.

Her new friends had to hide when her Daddy came in to say good night. They could see how much he loved his little girl. He tucked her in and kissed her good night, puzzled that, for once, she did not want to read her favorite book.

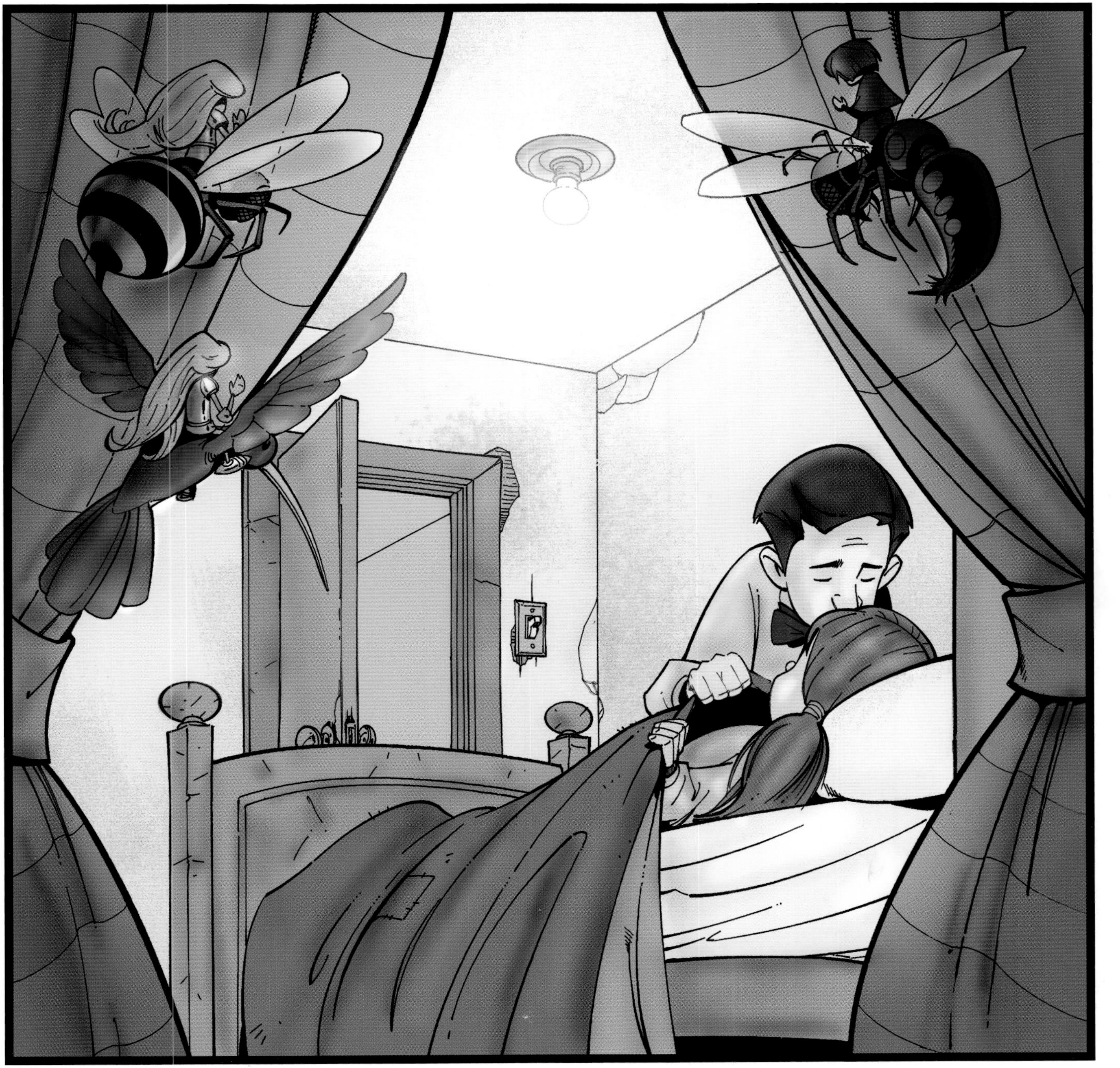

After Tammy went to sleep, Frankie, Sasha and the Formerly Mean Queen stayed up talking and made a secret plan to help her before they left. After all, that's what friends do, isn't it? Help each other?

The next morning, Tammy went to school. Frankie, Sasha and the Formerly Mean Queen followed her, amazed at this very enormous and very different world.

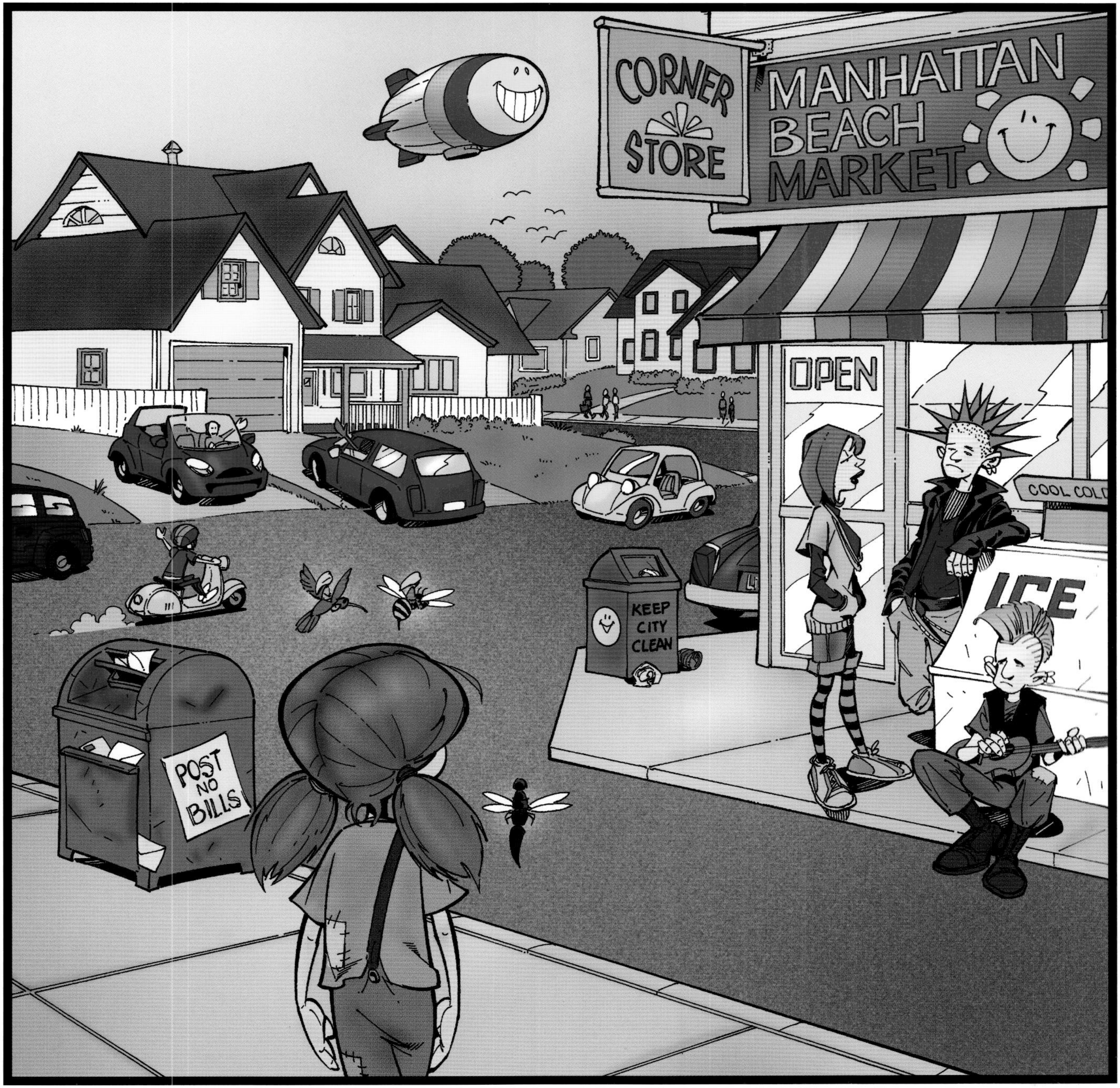
CORNER STORE
MANHATTAN BEACH MARKET
OPEN
COOL COLD
ICE
KEEP CITY CLEAN
POST NO BILLS

Soon, they were in the schoolyard. A boy saw them and began to walk their way.

"Oh, no! That's Max!" Tammy said nervously.

"Be brave, and remember your friends are here," whispered Frankie in her left ear.

"You are stronger than you know, Tammy," whispered Sasha in her right ear.

Max looked like a cute little boy from a distance, but up close, he was nothing but mean and nasty. He blocked the walkway.

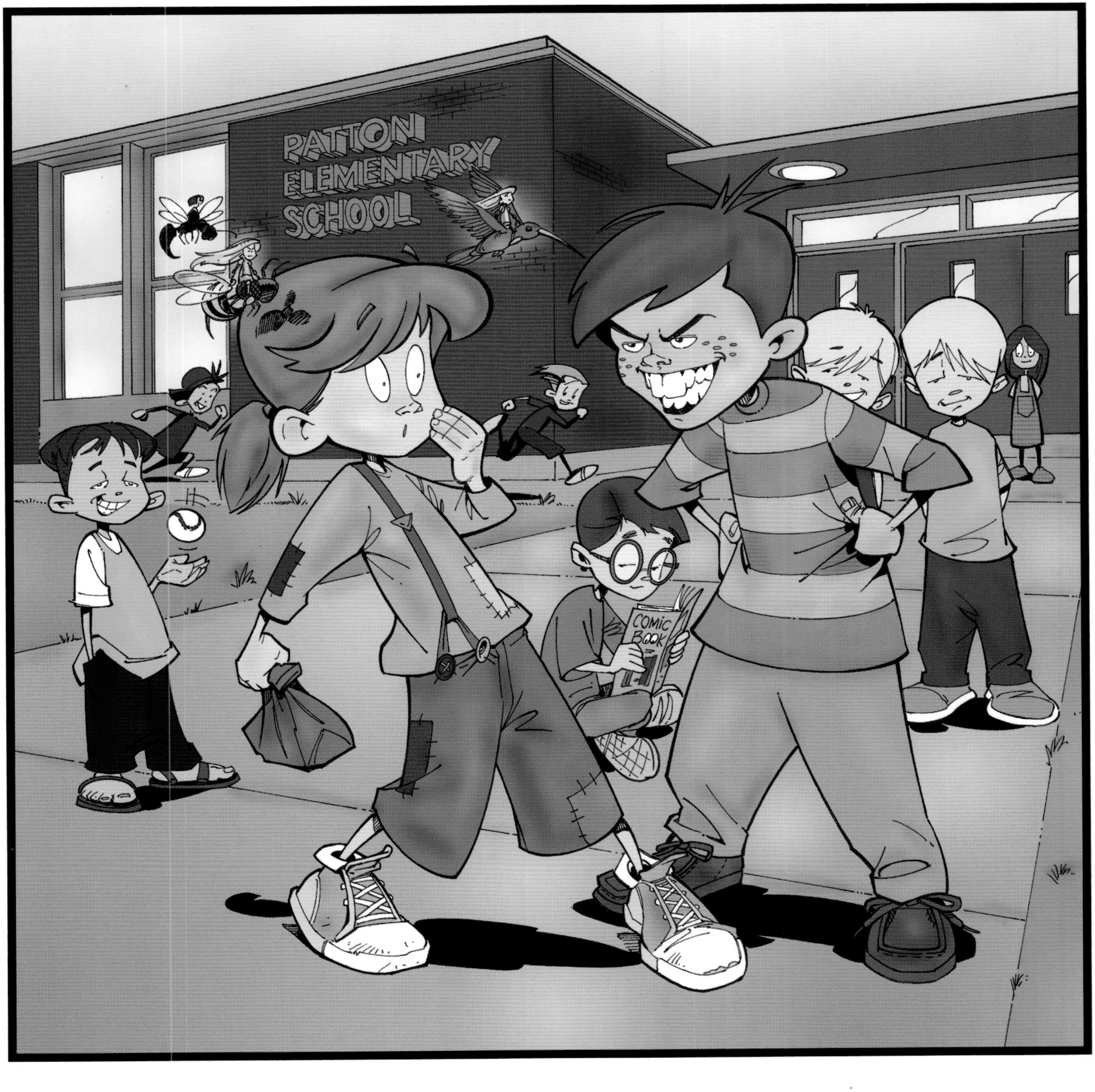
PATTON ELEMENTARY SCHOOL
COMIC BOOK

"Hello, you stinky old turnip," he sneered, and reached out to pull her hair. Tammy quickly stepped back. He grabbed her lunch, and she grabbed it right back. A flicker of surprise and doubt appeared in his beady little eyes. And then bad things happened.

A hummingbird swooped down and landed on his nose. It was wearing armor and looked mad! A tiny girl was riding it. She pointed a sword right at his eye!

"Young man, you will never bother Tammy again. Never! Do you understand?"

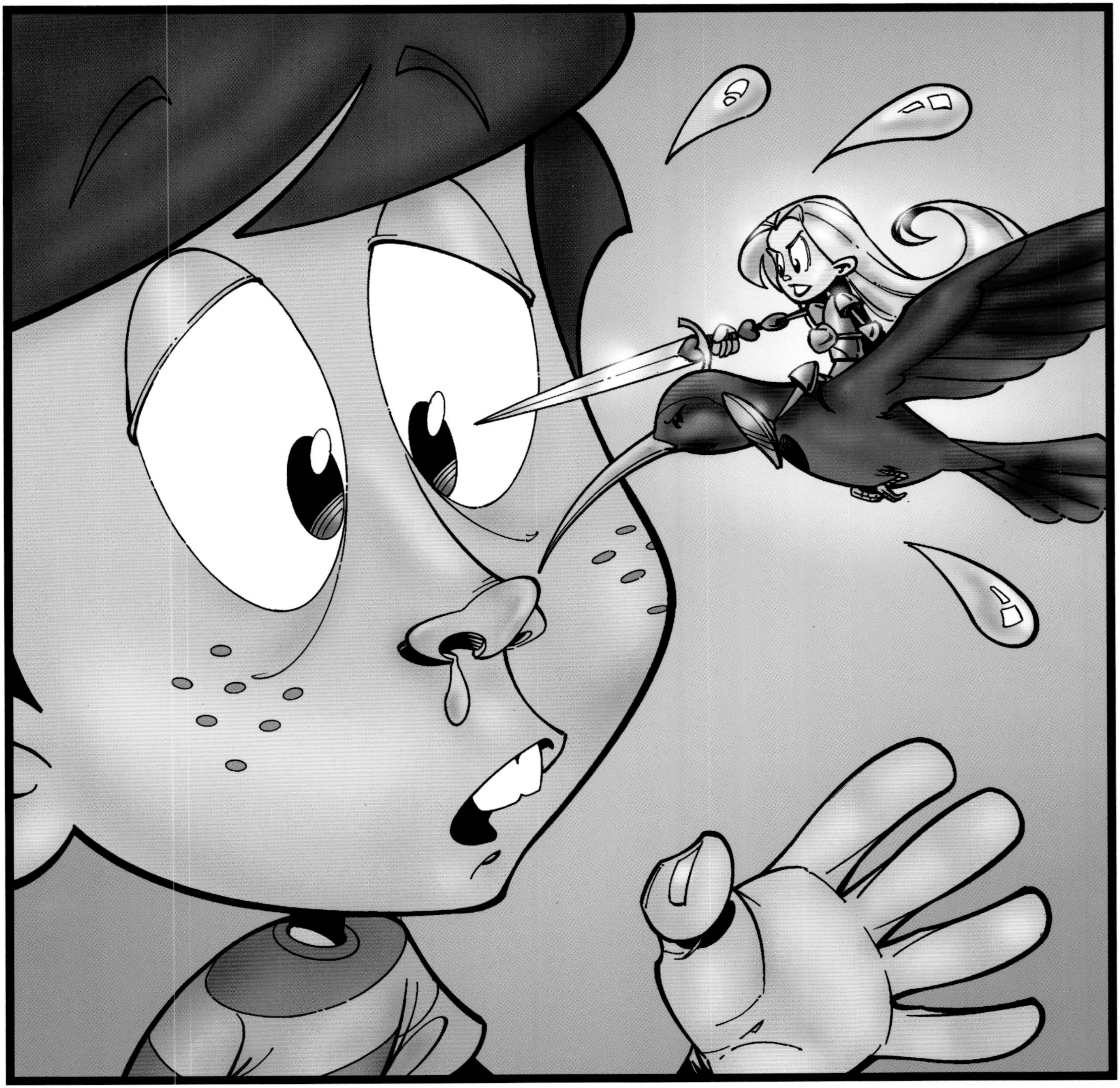

Max was beginning to nod a "yes" when Frankie's bumble-bee and the Formerly Mean Queen's wasp stung him on the behind. Twice.

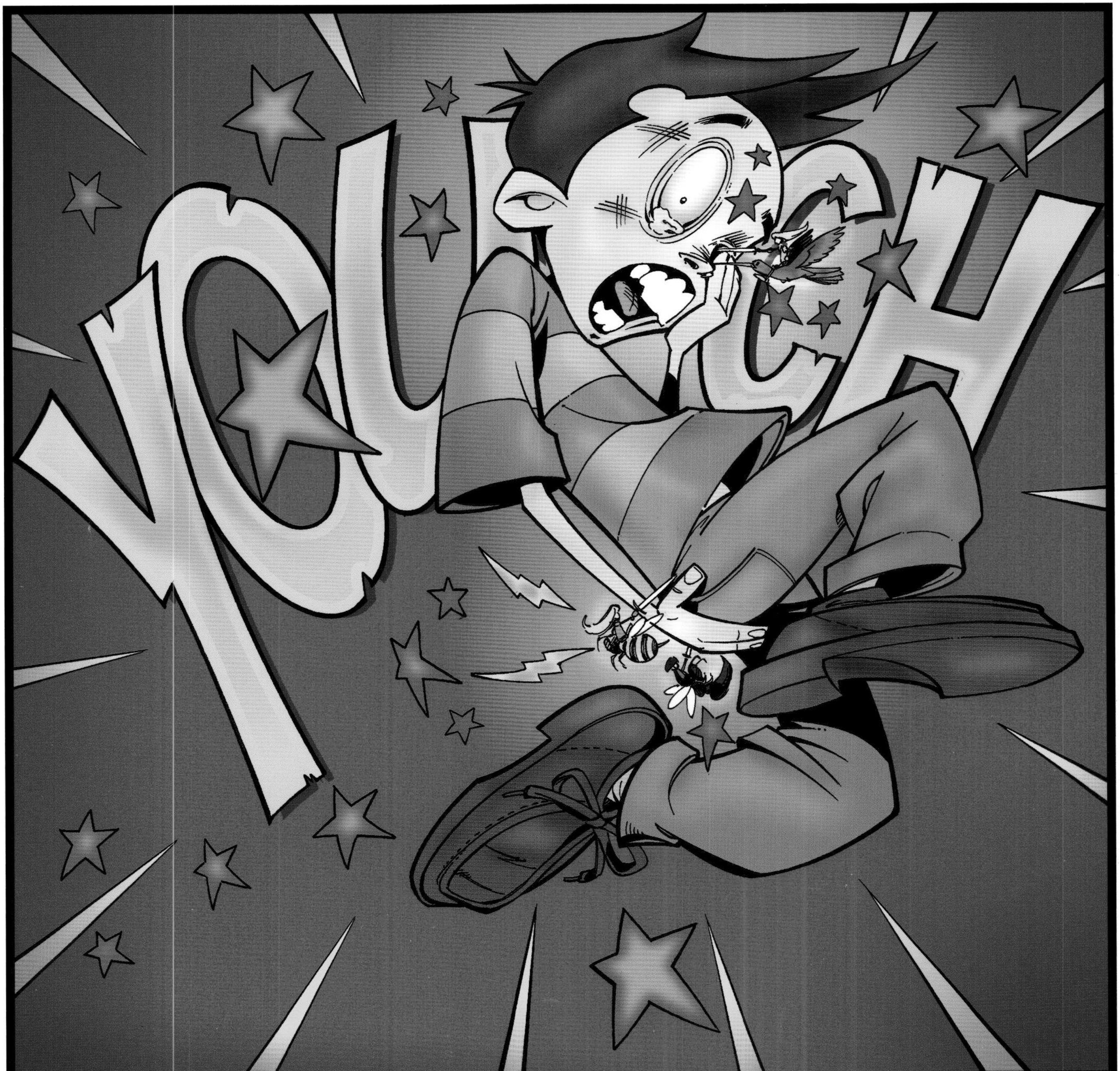
YOUCH

"Youch!" Max yelled and took off running. It hurt so badly, and it was getting worse! He finally sat himself down in a big mud puddle to soothe his throbbing rear end. All the other kids pointed and laughed at him as he sat there in the mud and cried. Tammy didn't join in. Just because Max was mean to her didn't make it okay for her to be mean to him.

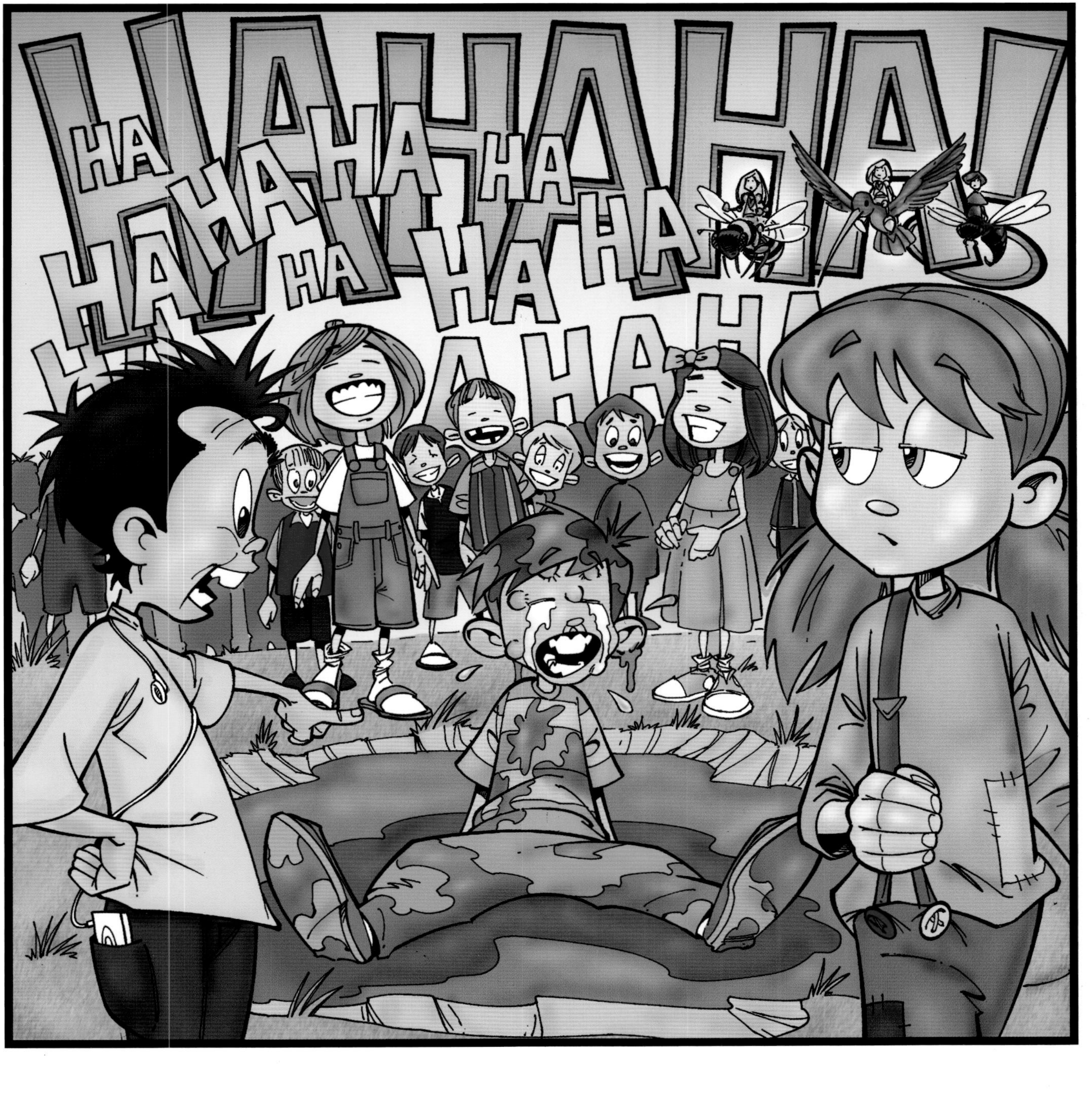

HAHAHA!
HA
HA HA HA HA
HA
HA HA
HA
HA HA
HA HA HA

Soon, the word spread about how Tammy stood up to Max and made him cry. Pretty soon, everyone in the school knew about it! All the other girls and boys that Max had picked on thought that Tammy was very brave and told her so. Tammy made many friends that day.

That night, the Formerly Mean Queen studied her book of spells.

"I think I can get us back, but I will need an object that contains a great amount of the good kind of magic to do it." She looked sad. "Where will we find any kind of magic in this world?"

Tammy thought about it for a minute. A long time ago, when she was just a baby, her Daddy carved an angel to watch over her. He used wood from the tree that he had met her Mommy under.

"My Daddy always says there is nothing in this world stronger than his love for me and that it will always be that way forever. Isn't that magic?"

The others all agreed, of course, that it was and every bit as powerful as any HooHooHaHa magic. Tammy took the angel from over her bed and laid it down next to them.

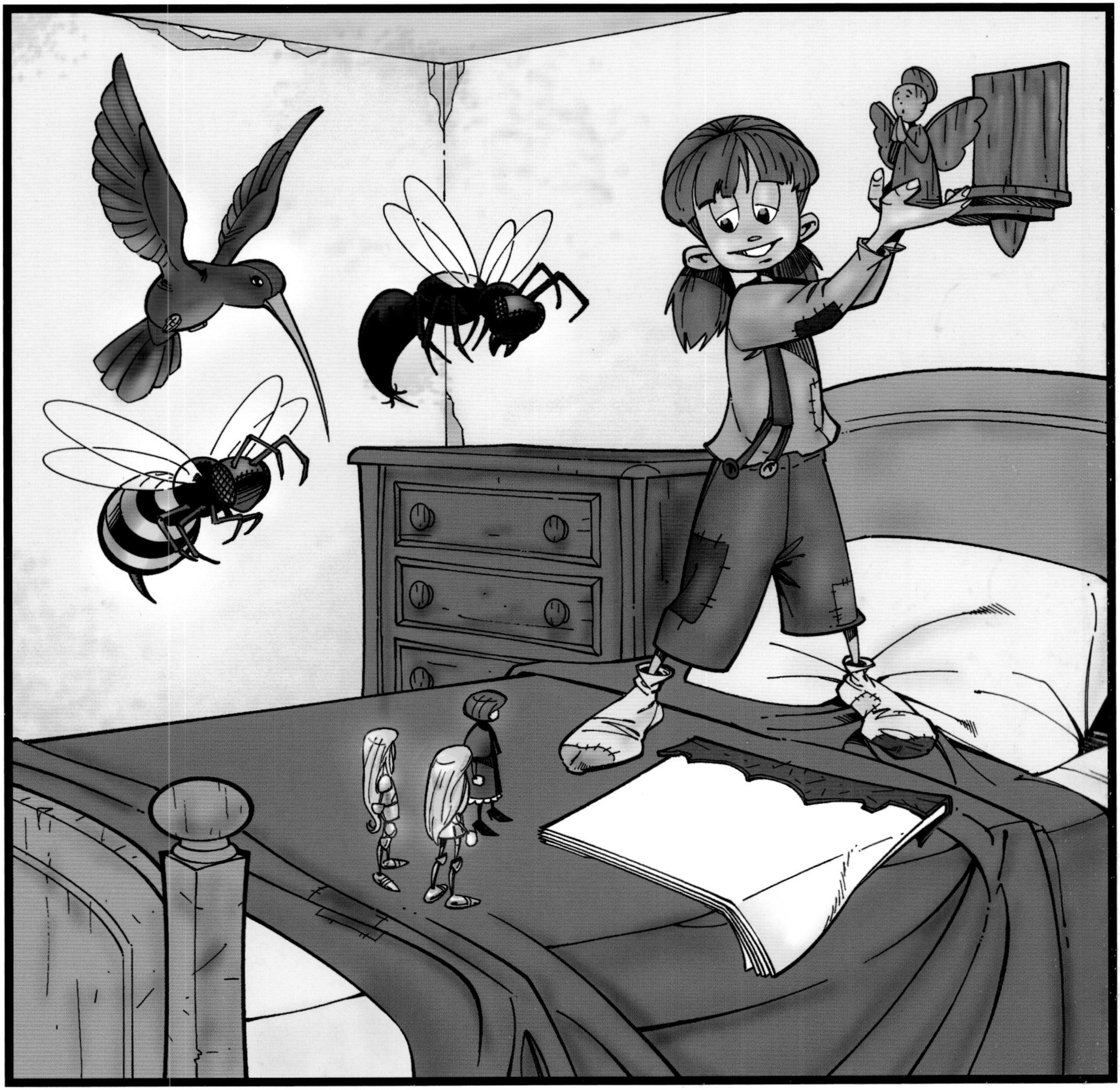

The Formerly Mean Queen cast the spell. The book opened up. They all kissed Tammy goodbye and flew back into the book. Once the Princesses and the Formerly Mean Queen were safely inside, the book slammed shut, magically looking as good as new!

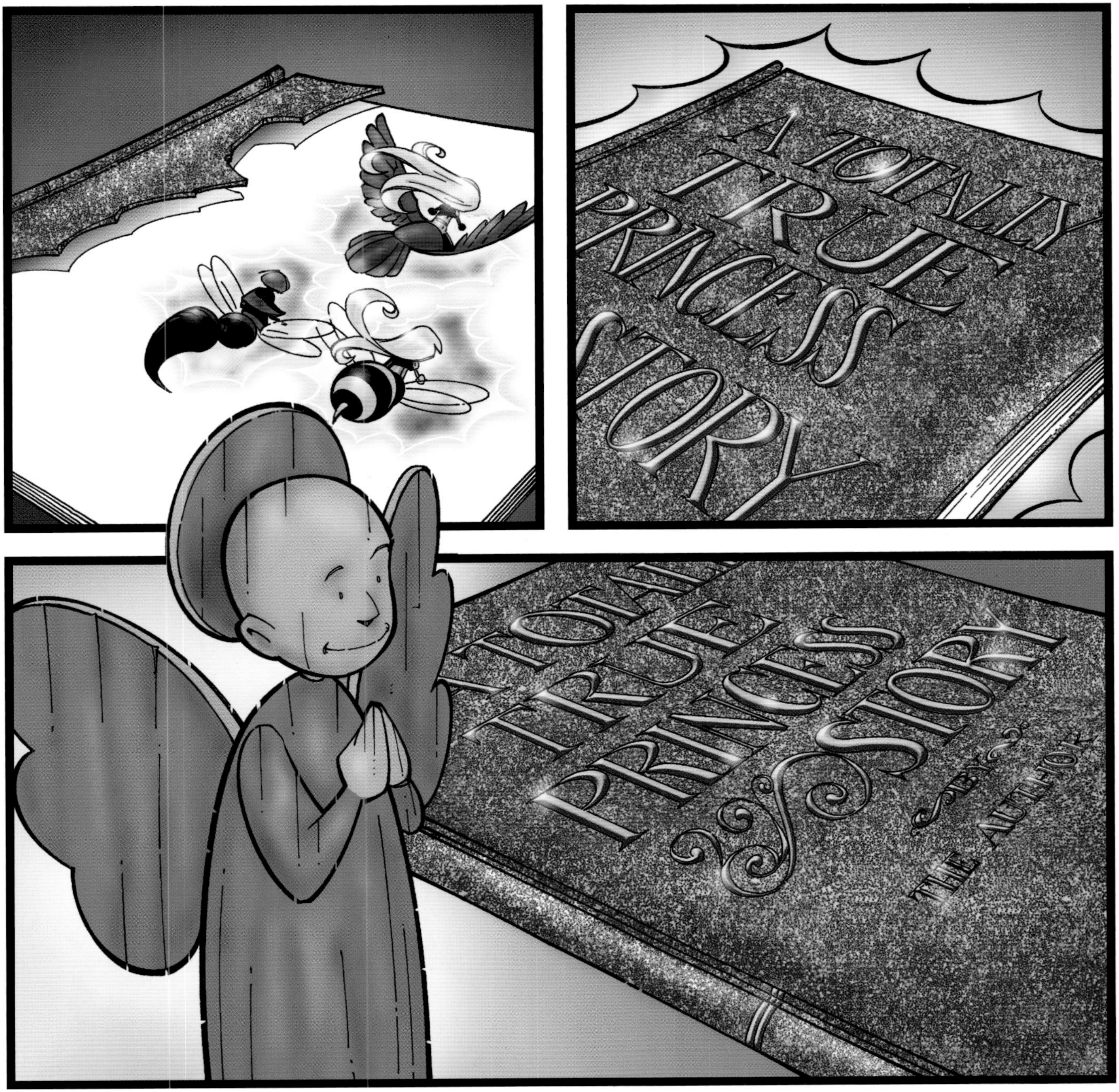
A TOTALLY TRUE PRINCESS STORY
A TOTALLY TRUE PRINCESS STORY
BY
THE AUTHOR

Suddenly, there was a loud scream. Tammy ran into the living room just in time to see the babysitter magically transformed into a snorting pig-girl!

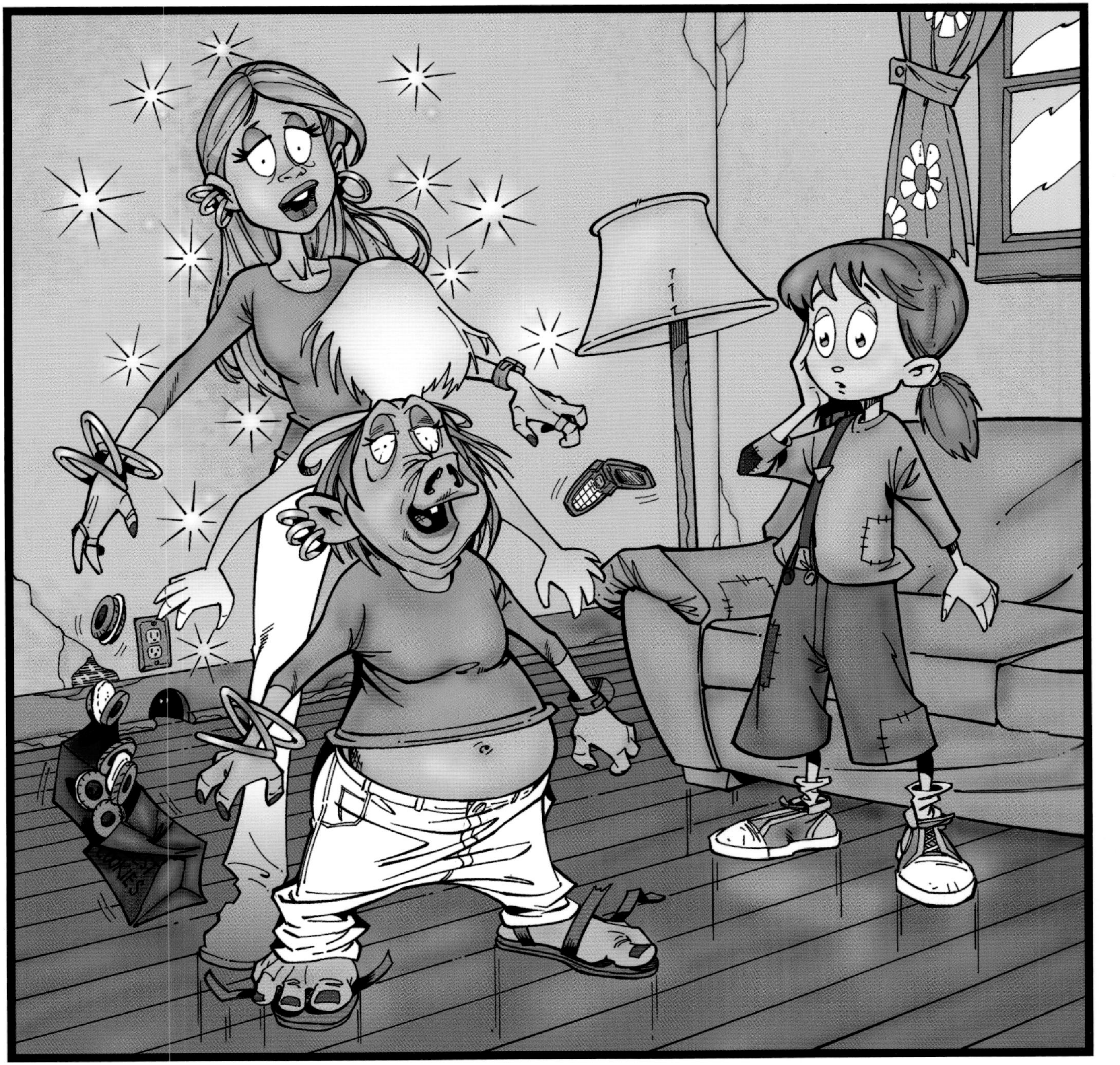

You see, the first part of the secret plan Frankie, Sasha and the Formerly Mean Queen had made was to punish the babysitter for being so awful to Tammy. So they made her as ugly on the outside as she was on the inside. She opened the door and ran away screaming (although it actually sounded more like oinking) through her new pig snout as she ran out of the house.

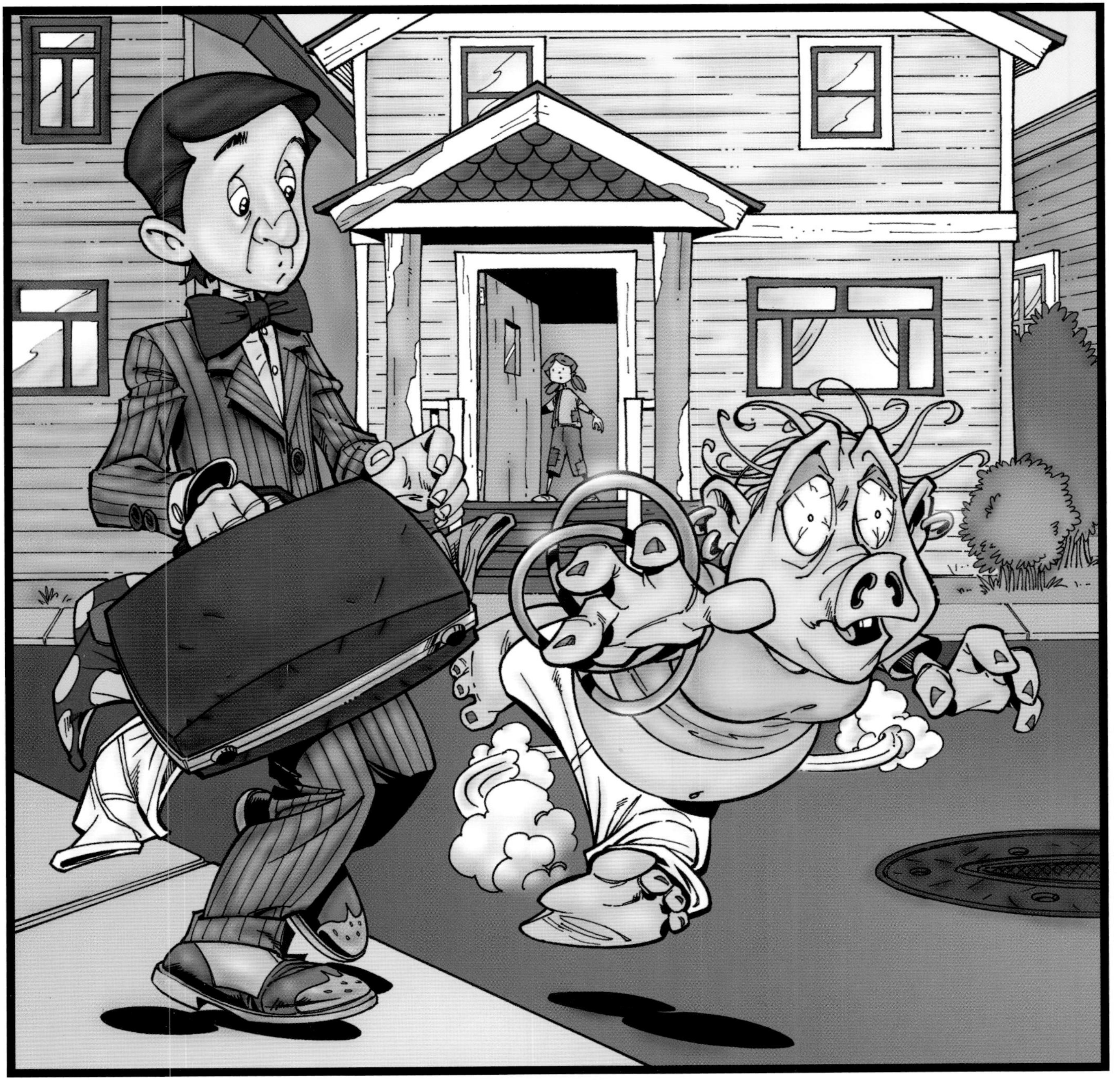

She passed Mr. Turnipseed on the sidewalk. He was coming home early to tell Tammy the good news. He had just been promoted to the head of the factory!

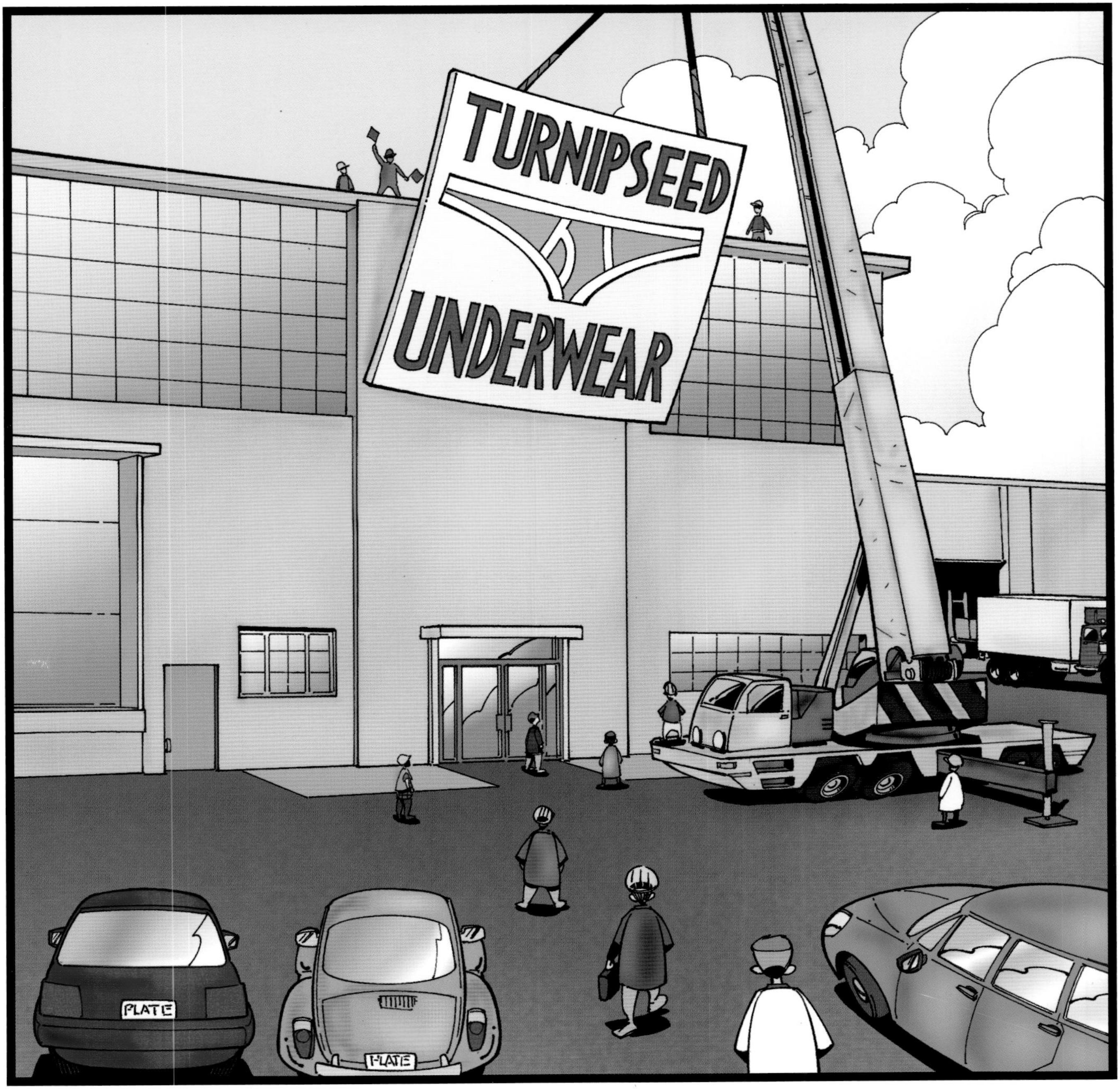
TURNIPSEED
UNDERWEAR
PLATE
PLATE

This was the second part of the secret plan. Mr. Turnipseed would make more money, enough for new clothes and a nicer babysitter for Tammy. Also, he wouldn't have to work late at night or on weekends anymore.

A few days later, on a play date, Mr. Turnipseed met the mother of one of Tammy's new friends. They fell in love and got married soon thereafter. Now, Tammy had a new sister named Cindy and a new Mommy too! That wasn't part of the secret plan, it just happened.

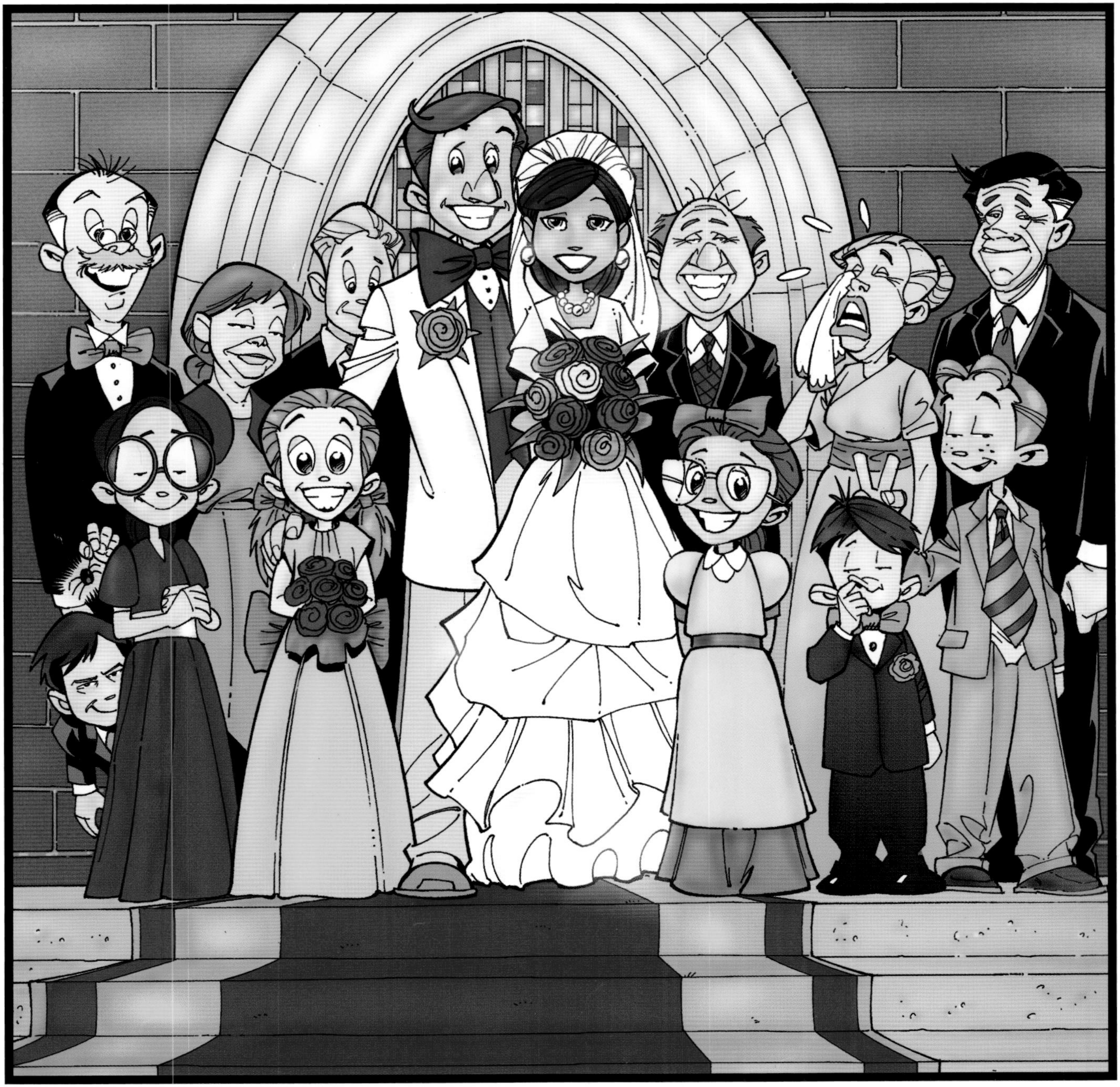

Now, Mommy and Daddy would snuggle in bed with Tammy and Cindy and the book. They all loved it because now it was a different story every time they read it. And if they weren't too busy in the story, sometimes the Princesses would even wave at them!

And one time, Tammy and Cindy visited HooHooHaHa and saved the kingdom… but that is a story for another day.

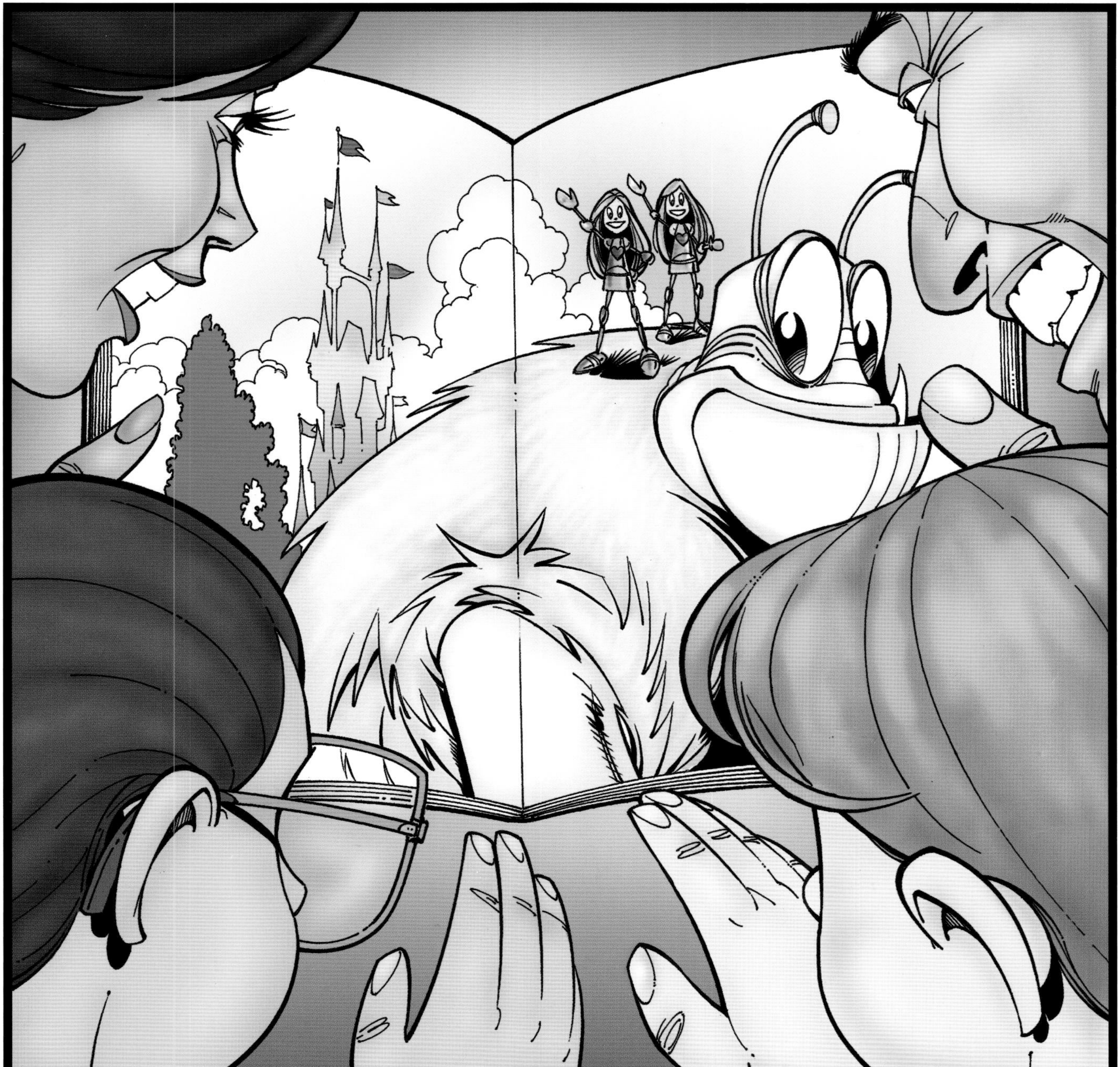

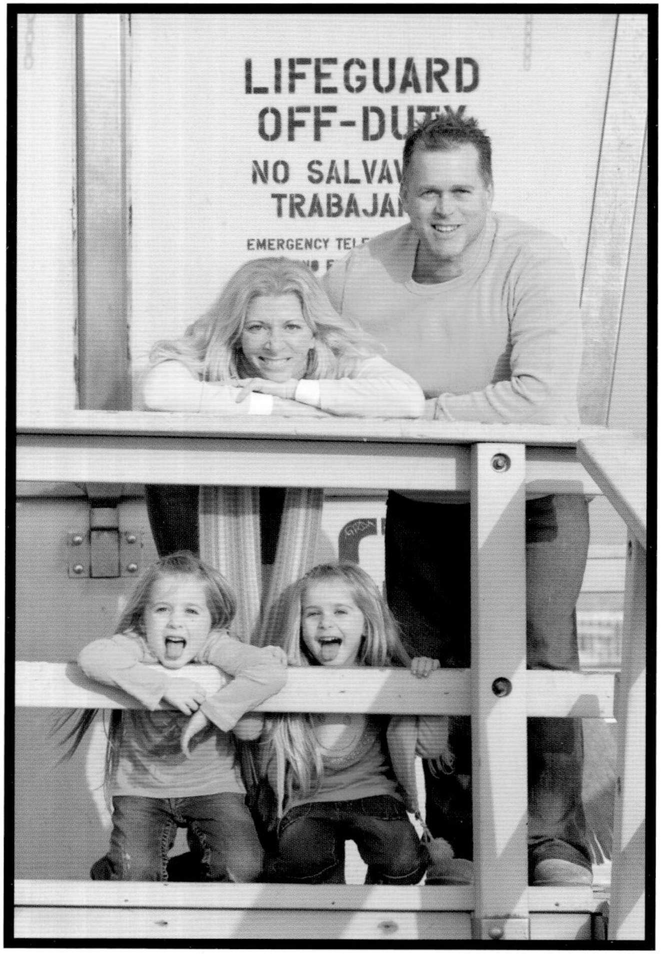
LIFEGUARD
OFF-DU
NO SALVAV
TRABAJA
EMERGENCY TEL

About the Author:

Chris Patton lives with his Queen and Two Princesses in Manhattan Beach, California.